MW00899228

To Steal a Highlander's Heart

SAMANTHA HOLT

Copyright © 2013 Samantha Holt

All rights reserved.

ISBN: 1492290378
ISBN-13: 978-1492290377

CONTENTS

ACKNOWLEDGMENTS

A big thank you to Eileen for ensuring I stayed true to her Scottish heritage and answering all my silly questions. I must also thank Joy who has helped me out with countless books and continues to tolerate endless emails of nonsense as I work things out. I also owe Sue lots of love and thank yous. You've been a huge support to me and I will always be grateful that I 'met' you. I will love you always.

PROLOGUE

Moray, Scotland 1230

Morgann grimaced as floorboards creaked and he paused and listened. He swallowed, the sound loud in his ears but he heard no one approach, no heavy footsteps pounding up the stairs. Beneath him, the feast continued. Raucous shouts and laughter rang out. He slipped across the solar, skirted the wide blue bed and paused in front of a carved chest. It had to be in here. He'd snuck into the laird's chambers with Alana enough times and they both knew her father kept his most precious belongings in there.

Crouching, he lifted the lid, gently resting it back. Furs and blankets hid the box but he managed to find it even in the dim moonlight. He freed the small silver box, stood and held it up to the window. *Damnation*. It was locked. He tried to pry it apart with his fingers but it refused to open.

He glanced around and sighed. Alana would probably come looking for him soon and he really didn't want to her to find out what he was doing. Having her think him a thief would be bad enough but he could not let her know the truth about her father. The lass loved him dearly.

Morgann shook his head. He wished Alana wasn't so trusting and sweet sometimes. Too often, she sought to see the best in people. Even him. And she forgave him far too readily for his flaws. She tolerated too much nonsense from him. Ach, what foolish talk. Alana was perfect. Sweet, understanding, funny and tolerant. Perfect wifely material.

He shook his head again and turned his attention back to the box. When a large burst of laughter sounded, he smashed the edge against the stone window ledge. The metal crumpled but refused to give way. He tried again and again. Finally the lid split from the base and he prized it apart. He grinned in triumph as he spotted what he'd been searching for.

His mother's ring.

Folding it into his fist, he felt the reassuring weight and considered with grim satisfaction what would happen to his stepmother now he'd found the ring that had supposedly been stolen. How would she explain how it happened to end up in Laird Dougall Campbell's hands?

Before he made his escape, a hand came upon his shoulder. He leaped around, fists ready but several men surrounded him.

Two pinned his arms behind him, stealing his chance at a fair fight and one plunged a fist into his stomach, forcing him to double over. He coughed and pulled himself up straight, straining against the hands that held him captive.

Laird Dougall pushed through the men and ran his gaze over him. Morgann cursed aloud as his hands were shackled behind him even as he fought to get free.

The grey-haired man loomed over him. "What are ye doing here, Morgann?"

"Getting what's mine," he snarled, unintimidated by Dougall's superior height. Though the man was one of the tallest Highlanders he knew, he was still aged and Morgann could take him in a fair fight.

"I knew ye were up to something. I could tell. Ye cannae fool me, MacRae. Ye've been looking at me like yer ready to slice my head off all eve."

A warrior pulled the ring from Morgann's palm and handed it over to Dougall. He lifted it and eyed it with a tight smile. "Been thieving have we?"

"That's my mothers and ye know it."

"But 'twas given to me. A gift."

Morgann clenched his jaw. "From a woman who has no rights over it. 'Twas a promise ring between my father and my mother. My stepmother should never have given it to ye."

Dougall laughed. "Yer stepmother gives me many things.

Quite a woman that one. I'll look forward to the day when she's mine."

"Yer welcome to her, but ye'll never get yer hands on MacRae lands too."

The older man's smile expanded as he clenched the ring. "So ye have me figured do ye? Yer a smart lad, Morgann. Too smart really. Ye'd have been better off just letting things run their course."

"And what happens when Alana finds out just what yer up to?"

Dougall's eyes narrowed. "My daughter is none of yer concern. Ye've always paid too much attention to her. Ach, I was even considering giving her to ye. Once I've married yer stepmother and taken yer lands, it seemed only right that ye at least have something."

"Alana will be heartbroken when she finds out what yer up to."

"As I told ye," Dougall ground out. "'Tis none of yer concern. I dinnae do this to hurt her. 'Tis the way of the world, lad. Surely ye can see that? If I want to be sure of providing her with all I can and the only way I can do that is by holding onto power. Ye wouldnae want to see her penniless now would ye?"

"That would never happen, Dougall. I wouldnae allow it."

"And I willnae allow ye to see her again. I'll no' have ye poisoning her against me. Yer banished from Dunleith. Ye and all the MacRaes." He stepped closer. "I love my daughter and I'll do all I can to protect her. Including keeping ye away from her. Ye step foot on my land again and ye'll be dead, understand?"

Releasing a growl, Morgann yanked at his restraints. His captors held him tight as he fought against their hold. Ach, but he'd failed. Failed to get the proof he needed and now he'd never get another chance. His gut burned with frustration.

"I'll no' let ye take the MacRae lands, Dougall." He yanked forward, throwing all his weight into the movement and the men's grip loosened enough for him to smash his head into Dougall's face. The man dropped to the floor, eyes wide as he clutched at a bloody nose.

Morgann's head pounded and he briefly saw stars but the men were upon him again, holding him tight. Dougall clambered to his feet and Morgann released a grin at the sight of blood streaming down his face.

"I tried to make it easy on ye, lad," Dougall pressed through gritted teeth. "Ye've only yerself to blame. Take him to the blacksmith's to be branded. He's a thief. He should be punished accordingly."

"*A mheapain!*" Morgann spat as the warriors dragged him across the room. Morgann was strong but no match for two fully grown men. He forced down the bile rising in his throat. He'd seen animals branded. The press of hot metal on skin would be excruciating.

To his shame they hauled him down the stairs and past the revellers, including some of his kin. He only hoped they were sent away peacefully and none decided to fight. They were sorely outnumbered. Alana rose from the table, a hand to her mouth as she watched them pass.

Morgann sagged into his captors' hold when they stepped out into the bailey. *Little use fighting now.* A feminine voice sounded behind him and they all paused.

"What are ye doing, Da?" Alana hurried across the mud, skirts in hand. "Why do ye hold Morgann prisoner? The MacRaes are baying for yer blood. I've told them Morgann must have been playing tricks again."

Dougall crossed his arms over his chest. "'Tis naught to do with ye, Alana. Go back inside. I'll deal with the MacRaes when I return."

She turned her gaze to Morgann. "Morgann?"

He swallowed. Funny, he'd never realised how pretty the lass was. Aye, she'd had her fair share of interest from suitors but there was something about her pale hair in the moonlight and the hint of womanly curves under her gown. And now her wide gaze latched onto his, begging for the truth.

He sighed. "Naught, Alana. 'Tis between us men. Go inside. I'll speak with ye soon and explain."

She nodded slowly, her brow still furrowed. "Aye, as ye will."

"Go now," her father commanded sharply.

Darting a look between both of them, Alana snatched her skirts once more. "Come to me later, Morgann."

A faint growl came from Dougall but the man clearly didn't want to upset his daughter so allowed Morgann to respond quietly, "Aye, later, lass."

As he was dragged to the blacksmith for his punishment, all hope fled and his heart sank. He doubted very much he'd ever see Alana again. And the future of his clan looked bleak indeed.

CHAPTER ONE

'Tis time the sidhe repay their debt, the faerie thought as she cracked open a shutter and peered at the sleeping woman. Aye, she was a pretty one. Not like herself, but beautiful enough. A plan had been hatched long ago but now was the time to put it into motion. Both were ready for it and if she did not take action soon, then there would be no going back. The fate of many souls rested in Tèile's hands. She smiled to herself as she flew up above the keep. The sleeping spell was ready. The woman's clan would not have the slightest clue what had happened. Her grin widened. She so enjoyed toying with humans.

***

Wisps of mist rose from the ground and swirled around

Alana's ankles. She thrust out a foot to watch the white haze dance about her before glancing over her shoulder at the keep in the distance. Tucked against the mountain and cut off by a shallow river, the tall stone castle seemed almost insignificant. She blew out a long breath and watched as it too misted.

Though pleased to be free from the keep, and her father's watchful eye, a sense of foreboding struck her. Alana frowned as she tried to recall why she had come out onto the moors. In truth, she barely remembered getting dressed yet here she was, in her pale blue plaid, hair braided, drawing in the early morning air. Only the foggy remnants of a dream remained, something that beckoned for her to come here.

And how was it there were no men to stop her from leaving?

A strange occurrence indeed, for her father never left the castle walls unattended. It had been deathly quiet. A morbid thought occurred to her and she wondered why she did not check that all was well. Had they been attacked overnight? Were her kinsmen dead? Nay, surely not, for there would be triumphant victors crowding the halls of Dunleith Keep by now and she would either be killed or captured.

The whole morning had been strange. Her first clear memory was standing in the moors and staring off into the distance as if awaiting something. A prickle danced over her skin and she spun wildly, feeling as though fingers had tickled down her spine. Ach, either someone played games with her or her mind was addled. She huffed. Too much time spent cloistered away.

Specks of orange sunlight filtered across the mountains, dancing between the cracks and valleys and Alana tilted her head. The urge to keep going, to see what lay over the other side warred within her. She so missed being outside, missed her freedom.

Da would have a fit.

With a sigh, she turned back to the castle, the stone tower seeming more grey and oppressive than ever before. Hitching up her skirts, she strolled leisurely back, taking her time to admire each wild flower as she went. She ought to walk quickly. Should her father discover her absence, he would no doubt lecture her on the dangers of her actions and would certainly remind her their enemies were everywhere. Ach, she saw no—

She spun wildly as the heavy thud of hooves sounded. A brown horse bore down upon her, barely a few paces away. Alana squeaked in surprise as the rider snatched her plaid and hauled her into the saddle in front of him, not even slowing the mount as he positioned her firmly in his arms. She scarcely comprehended how it had happened. One moment there had been no one and then suddenly... A ghost mayhap?

She tried to wriggle in his hold but a strong arm pinned her to his chest. "Release me, ye fool."

"I think not, my lady."

Alana scowled as the deep timbre of his voice singed through her, setting her senses on fire. There was something wildly disturbing yet familiar about it. Her heart hammered heavily as fear penetrated her surprise at being caught unawares. If he were an outlaw or an enemy clansmen she was as good as dead.

"Ye cannae kidnap me on my own lands!" she protested. "My da will have yer head, just ye see." Alana tried to keep her voice strong but even she heard the wobble in it.

"Be still," her captor commanded as she fought against his hold, the growing distance between her and the castle stealing her determination. "Ach, I told ye—"

The press against her chest loosened marginally and the world rushed past as she dropped to the ground. Dirt scraped across her face and hands as she tumbled along and a sharp pain slammed up her wrist as it jarred in an attempt to brace herself. The back of her head crashed into the ground and her vision clouded as she skidded to a stop.

Sweet Lord, was she dead? She ached everywhere. Alana blinked but the world remained out of focus. A shadow came across her and a jolt of panic flew through her. She attempted to turn onto her side but she could not. Her body refused to move.

"Alana?"

She blinked again, drawing in harsh, raspy breaths.

"Ye daft lass, ye could've killed yerself."

Who was this man and why was he lecturing her? What did he expect would happen when he tried to kidnap her? That she'd sit there like a mild and meek woman and play captive? And *how* did he know her name?

Vision clearing, she squinted up at the Highland warrior towering over her. Broad shouldered and thick through the chest, he peered at her down a long, hawk-like nose. Set in a strong jaw surrounded by too much dark stubble were firm lips, currently pulled into a twisted smile. Thick, black hair— *too much of that too*—curled at his neck, slightly shorter at the front.

Alana's jaw dropped. "Morgann MacRae."

He knelt, plaid stretching with the movement of his muscles, and touched a callused finger to her forehead. Heat pulsed through her skin and she flinched, the ache in her head pounding in response and making her wince.

"So ye do remember me."

"What are ye trying to do? Kill me?"

"Nay, 'twas not my intention. But yer the one who threw herself from a perfectly good horse."

She groaned as she attempted to sit and he flattened a hand to the back of her head, cradling it in his huge palm.

"I wouldnae jumped had ye no' snatched me. What are ye

playing at, ye great fool? I've no time for games, Morgann."

"Ach, 'tis no game I play, no' like when we were bairns. Anyway ye looked like ye had all the time in the world."

Aye, he was certainly no lad. Not anymore. The sweet lad from some eight summers ago was gone, replaced with a flesh and blood man. A raw, rough, handsome man. Her body pulsed in response to the predatory glimmer in his dark gaze.

"My da will be missing me," she said weakly, wincing as he pulled her to sitting.

He ignored her and thrust his thick fingers into her hair, probing her skull. She whimpered as he found a tender spot at the back of her head.

"Ye've a nasty bump. Are ye hurt anywhere else?"

Alana forgot to respond. That rough jaw sat a mere breath away as he knelt beside her and pressed his hands over her arms, checking for injuries. Morgann MacRae? She had not seen him in so long, not since…

"Ow!"

He released her wrist and cradled it carefully in his palm. "Forgive me. Yer wrist is swollen, can ye move it?"

I should swing it at his head, she thought, pleased to note some of her spirit had returned. Instead of voicing her discontent, she twisted her wrist and released a sharp hiss as throbbing pain ran through her arm.

"'Tis nae broken," Morgann concluded.

"How would ye know? Yer no healer."

His dark eyes clashed with hers, surrounded by thick black lashes. His gaze was intense and powerful and made her suddenly breathless. "I've seen enough injuries."

"Have ye?"

"Aye." He looked down but not before Alana noted the flicker of something painful in his eyes.

He drew his fingers down her side, prodding at her ribs. The shock of his touch through her clothing sent her rigid and dumb even though she knew she should be fighting him off or at least scolding him for such familiarity. It was the fall. Aye, that was it. It had stolen all sense from her.

"We must get ye aid, ye've taken a nasty tumble and I think yer a wee addled."

"I am not addled!"

His lips quirked. "Well yer no docile lass, I'll give ye that."

Before she could protest, he'd scooped her into his arms and lifted her over to his waiting mount. His solid chest pressed to hers, the rough fabric of his plaid rubbing under her palm and the undulation of muscles made her head swim. Eyes wide, she gaped up at the man who stood in the place of her childhood friend. Ach, mayhap she was addled

***

Morgann tensed his jaw as Alana's soft body chafed against

him and that doe-eyed green gaze settled on his face. Hell fire, she had taken him by surprise. Aye, she'd been a bonny lass but he'd never thought just eight years would have her growing into such a fine creature. A willowy figure, glossy golden hair the colour of the sunset and a delicate face with a stubborn pointed chin. Aye, very bonny. He flicked his gaze to her lips and the rest of his body tensed too. Those lips were currently pursed into a pout of dissatisfaction but it did not disguise their succulence.

Hell fire.

She stiffened as he ordered his mount to lower. "Ye cannae take me to my da, he'll have yer head."

"I've little intention of taking ye to yer da or losing my head."

Morgann climbed onto his chestnut mare, Caraid, and settled Alana across his lap. She cradled her sore wrist and it was clear she was in more pain than she'd revealed. Stubborn lass. Ach, but he was a fool. He didn't even know what had come over him when he'd seen her, only that this was his one opportunity to finally reveal the truth and by God he was going to take it.

Why exactly had he been trespassing on Dunleith land again? He frowned as he tried to recall.

"What are ye planning to do with me, Morgann?"

He liked the way his name rolled off her tongue. Sweet like honey, yet spicy and inviting. What was he planning to do with her anyway? Ransom her? Mayhap. Or at least use her as a bargaining tool. Or keep her forever…

He shrugged off the thought. *Fool.* If he was to ever reveal the truth to his father, he needed every advantage. Even if it meant kidnapping the Laird of Dunleith's daughter.

"I'll take ye to Glencolum. We'll get ye back to full health there."

She wriggled against his hold but her injuries must have weakened her and now he was ready for a fight, he held her easily.

"Ye *were* trying to kidnap me!" she exclaimed with a huff of frustration.

He shrugged as he directed the horse northwards to Glencolum Keep and his family lands. Back to safety.

"Ye, Morgann, are naught but a lowlife criminal. A barbarian scoundrel. Return me home, ye bloody fool. Ye'll be beheaded for this, just ye see. My da will come get me and he'll kill all of ye. Ye and yer kinsmen. Put me down!"

Morgann grunted as a pointy elbow connected with his stomach. "Keep still. Yer lucky ye didnae kill yerself with that fall. I dinnae want to be returning ye to yer da in pieces."

In truth, he didn't want to be returning her harmed at all. The lass was fortunate she'd not done any real damage. A sprained wrist and a bump to the head was naught compared to what could have occurred. But, by God, she was spirited.

What happened to the sweet little lassie he'd known? Insulting him? She'd never have done that before.

"Be still," he tried again as her bottom wriggled against him. He bit back a grunt. He'd not had a woman in far too long. She had no idea what kind of trouble she was getting herself into. "Alana, if ye dinnae be still, I swear I'll put ye over my knee."

She gasped. "Ye wouldnae!"

"I would."

"Ach, I dinnae believe ye. Ye always said a man who beat a woman was no man at all. I remember," she replied smugly.

Hell, she had him there. What else did the lass remember? What else did she know? He'd not seen her since that night when the tentative peace between the MacRaes and the Campbells had ended. All thanks to him.

She'd asked him how he knew her wrist wasn't broken. Well, he had seen many injuries far more grievous than a sprained wrist in the years since. The fighting had been brutal and bloody. Now both clans kept their distance, afraid of any more losses. Both too stubborn and proud to even think of forgetting the past hurts. Not that he would ever forgive Dougall Campbell. Aye, he'd left them well enough alone recently but given the chance the man would snatch his lands from underneath him.

Ignoring her pointed statement, he kept his focus on the ragged horizon. And not on the supple little body pressing into him. Nay, he wouldn't think on that and how perfect she felt.

He gave Caraid a light kick with his heels. He needed to get to Glencolum as quickly as possible. And it was not fear of the Campbells catching up that drove him.

***

Tèile grimaced as she wriggled in the saddle bag of the Highland warrior. It was hot and cramped and certainly not fit for a faerie. And they were making quick progress. Far too quick. Before long they would be back at the keep and around others. The boorish humans would never allow them a chance for love to blossom. If only she was allowed to meddle with their hearts. Unfortunately human hearts were beyond the reach of faeries. But no matter, she would implant a few dreams next time they slept. First she needed to slow them down.

Peeking out of the top of the leather satchel, she glanced at the skies. No sign of even the slightest rain. The clear sky with its puffy white clouds was sickeningly devoid of interesting weather. Well, she would soon change that. A few muttered words and the grey clouds rolled in.

Ha, let's see if that would not slow them down.

CHAPTER TWO

Alana watched the sky darken with apprehension. This day had gone from mildly confusing to outrageously strange. *Kidnapped, thrown from a horse, kidnapped again.* And now it looked as though they were about to be caught up in the most sudden storm she'd ever witnessed in her three and twenty summers.

"Morgann..." She shifted so she could see him out of the corner of her eye.

He glanced down, pinning her with his powerful gaze.

"There looks to be a storm."

"Aye, I can see that."

"Should we not stop?"

"And where, pray tell, should we stop?"

"I know not. But I dinnae want to get wet."

And she wanted a chance to escape again but she wouldn't mention that part. Ach, her first taste of freedom in years and she'd been kidnapped. She certainly wasn't going to let herself be taken prisoner. The MacRaes *hated* the Campbells. Who knew what was in store for her? But for the moment her head hurt too much to put up a real fight and she really did not want to fall from the mount again. Let him think she would cooperate for the moment. Mayhap he would let down his guard and give her a chance to escape.

Fat heavy drops began to fall, pattering against the grey rocks strewn across the hills and soaking through her clothing. Morgann cursed into her hair but continued to push his mount on through the valley as the leaden clouds converged about the mountains, washing the scenery with ominous shadows.

In the distance the heavy rumble of thunder sounded, making Alana shiver. The steady rainfall leached through to her skin, increasing the quaking of her body until her teeth chattered and Morgann cursed once more and eased her into his torso.

His chest provided some warmth. More than she wanted to think about really. She'd always admired him when they were younger but she did not need to be nursing an attraction to him while he kidnapped her. If he succeeded in taking her back to Glencolum Keep, the tension between the two clans would ignite and Highland blood would paint the hills red.

Nay, that could not be allowed to happen. Her father suffered with his health. No longer a great Highland warrior, war surely meant death for him. Alana loved him dearly, in spite of his flaws. Da was determined to still be seen as a man of great strength and power and who could blame him? But his warmongering ways spelled trouble for their entire clan. Since that day eight summers ago, life had been fraught with danger and she'd been confined to the keep.

A shudder wracked her again and she acquiesced to the warm strength of Morgann's body. She needed to try and retain her strength if she wanted to escape his clutches. And *of course* she wanted to.

She tensed. *Did he just hiss?* She squeezed her eyes shut and tore them open once more, hoping the strange fog of—*of need?*—had gone. *Concentrate.* Taut muscles rippled against her back as he guided the horse skilfully between the rock-strewn hills. *Not on that, Alana!* She blew out a heavy breath. She needed to think of anything other than the sensation of a powerful male body flattened against her.

Well, she had taken a hit to the head. And it had been a while since she'd spent time in the company of any man other than her kinsmen. None were as handsome as Morgann to be sure.

Ach, handsome as he was, he was still abducting her.

She stole a peek over her shoulder. Of course, he'd always been attractive but she had never envisaged him turning into this... this beast of a man. Had the years changed everything? He'd certainly lost his playful countenance she remembered from their time together. Was it just hidden or gone? His dark eyes now had a haunted look to them. But what did she expect after what her father had done to him? She still regretted not being able to speak with him afterwards. Still regretted not getting the chance to tell him that she believed in him.

The heavy boom of thunder grew closer, echoing across the valley and Alana shrank back into Morgann's hold.

"Ach, we must stop," Morgann muttered in her ear, making her jolt as his breath whispered over her. "The ground is soaked. I risk hurting Caraid."

Alana sniffed. Wonderful. He cared more for the horse's welfare than hers. Still, she'd not complain. Mayhap she could at least talk him out of taking her to his keep. Or just escape. Morgann did seem very determined and that brooding look in his eyes made her stomach twist in apprehension.

They approached a jutting rock at the base of a mountain and he directed Caraid over and slid from the saddle. Alana prepared to jump down but before she made a move his large hands were upon her, gliding her down his body. A rush of blood pounded through her head and their gazes connected for the merest moment. As slight as it was, the instant made her stomach flutter and she suspected those eyes would haunt her dreams for many nights.

"Rest awhile under that rock while I—"

As Morgann turned from her to grab the mount's reins,

Alana slipped past. She hadn't even planned the move, but now seemed as good a time as any. She made to run but something snagged her gown and she slipped on the wet ground, landing face first into the mud. She rolled and fought to come to her feet, but it was Morgann that had a hold of her skirts.

He cursed as she wriggled and struck out at him with a foot. "Be still," he commanded as he attempted to seize her leg.

"Nay!" she shouted as she planted her foot in his middle and scrabbled away. "I'll no' let ye take me."

But he was swiftly upon her, this time using his full weight to pin down her legs. No matter how much she thrashed, she was no match for his brutal strength. Morgann slid up her until she was trapped completely beneath him.

"Damn ye, Morgann," she hissed as he pressed the breath from her with his body.

Alana swiped at him but he curled a hand around one wrist, then the other, making her wince, and trapped them above her. Heavy breaths blew across her skin as he glared at her, nostrils flaring.

She gulped and gave another wriggle. The strongly clenched jaw, the anger in his eyes made her stomach tighten. She didn't know this man, she realised. The playful friend she had once known had been replaced by a dangerous warrior. One intent on capturing her.

"Let me go," she said feebly, biting back a whimper as her

wrist throbbed. She attempted to draw her hands from his grip. "Yer hurting me."

The grip tightened. "Cease yer fighting, lass. Yer going nowhere."

"Never," she spat. "I'll no' let ye use me as a pawn in yer power games."

"Ye think this is about power?" He laughed dryly. "Alana, I have no wish to take land or start wars. But ye must come with me. 'Tis the only way."

Tired and confused, Alana relaxed against his hold. If he didn't wish to barter her for a chance at some of her father's land, then what did he want with her? What other reason was there for taking an enemy's daughter? Revenge mayhap?

"What do ye want me for then?"

"Will ye cease fighting me if I explain?"

"Aye."

The hold around her hands released as he watched her closely. But she knew better than to fight him. It didn't mean she'd stop trying to escape. Nay, she just had to choose her moment more carefully. The warrior was obviously determined to take her.

She made the mistake of holding his gaze as he made to climb off and her chest tightened. He paused and they stared at each other. Emotion simmered behind his gaze, the anger gone, and Alana couldn't tell if the emotion was targeted at her or something else. All she knew was the feeling of having his strong weight on top of her, his gaze boring into her, stole all sensible thought and turned her into one quivering mass of sensations.

Endless moments stretched on as she waited for Morgann to look away, to break the connection, but he stared brazenly on as his gaze trailed over her face. What did he see? As she gaped up at him, the irate warrior dissolved into a flesh and blood man and she recalled how much she used to adore him. When Morgann was banished from her father's lands, she'd been heartbroken at losing her friend, but with the blazing sensation of having him flattened against her, she remembered it wasn't just the loss of his friendship that hurt her so. She'd always silently hoped Morgann would play a bigger role in her future.

But that didn't change the fact he was taking her against her will and she would not go meekly, regardless of what she once felt for him. She wouldn't put herself and her clan in danger all because they'd once been friends. If only she could ignore the sensuous pull of his lips or the darkening of his pupils as a rough finger drew a path over her cheek.

A crack ripped across the sky and they both jolted. Pushing to standing, Morgann helped her up and grimaced as he eyed her. Aware of the mud coating her, she swiped a hand across her face as her cheeks heated. Tilting her head up, she hoped the rain would at least be useful for something and not only rinse away some of the dirt but also cool her down. The way the man made her skin blister was extremely disconcerting.

Morgann muttered a curse, drawing her attention back to him as he raked a hand through his hair and yanked some rope from the leather pouch hanging from his saddle. As he turned back to her, rope held out, Alana shrank away.

"Ye cannae mean to tie me up, surely?"

"'Tis clear ye cannae be trusted. I'll no' have ye escaping me again."

She pressed herself back as he approached her cautiously. "I thought ye were going to tell me of yer plans, not tie me up. If I'd have known ye planned that, I'd have fought harder."

"I dinnae doubt it. Why do ye think I agreed to tell ye?"

Licking her lips, Alana darted her gaze around, looking for an escape. If he tied her up, all hope would be lost. "So ye dinnae plan to tell me aught?"

"I dinnae take pleasure in this, Alana, but I'll no' see ye harmed." He grabbed a wrist as she attempted to dodge his reach. "I just need ye for a while."

Why did those words send a flutter of excitement to her toes? She tried to run past him and tear herself from his grip but a strong arm came around her waist and held her back as he coiled the rope around one wrist.

"Ye say ye dinnae want to hurt me, yet ye intend to tie me up like a common prisoner?"

As he opened his mouth to argue, the mare whinnied and they both turned to see her rear.

"Damnation!" Morgann dropped the rope and snatched at the reins but it was too late, the horse bolted. He immediately gave chase and Alana watched for a moment as he sprinted after the frightened mare.

She stole a quick peek at the skies and uttered a thank you. Hopefully she could evade Morgann in the rocky landscape and find her way home. They hadn't journeyed too far though she'd never travelled these lands unaccompanied and the last time she'd visited Morgann's home was many years ago.

And she was definitely on enemy land.

Nerves beat in her chest but she shoved the sensation aside and fell into a run. She deliberately followed the base of the mountains, snaking in and out of the protruding rocks, some bigger than a cottage, having tumbled down the peaks long ago. If he managed to catch up with his mount quickly, then mayhap the rocks would hide her for long enough to gain some distance.

The rain continued to fall and her plaid grew heavy and cumbersome. It provided little warmth now it was soaked so she unpinned it and let it fall from her shoulders. Aye, mayhap she risked freezing to death but she didn't plan on being out in the wilderness for long. Soon she'd be back home by the warmth of a fire. She thrust a hand out and used a rock to help her navigate the slippery surface of the mountain, stifling a shudder.

Aye, just think on that, Alana. A warm fire. Heavy blankets. Some heated wine. An unbidden image of Morgann pressed on top of her, warming her in other ways burst through her thoughts. Where had that come from? She was old enough to know of the pleasure that could be shared between a man and a woman. And wise enough to realise that it would likely be extremely pleasurable sharing that with Morgann but she'd never had these sort of heated imaginings before, only simple ideas more suited to that of an inexperienced maiden.

Alana's foot slipped from under her and only her grip on the rock stopped her from falling into the mud again. She made her way higher up the mountain after glancing at the valley below. She saw no sign of Morgann. If he caught up with his mount, he would stick to the valley paths and with any luck wouldn't see her so high up.

What a fool she was for stepping outside the keep. Da had been right. Since the rift between the two clans, both families' lands were dangerous. She just never expected Morgann to be the one to attempt such an exploit. If she was very unlucky, other Glencolum men would be prowling the lands and she may end up in even bigger trouble. None would treat her with much more care.

She still found it hard to believe that sweet Morgann wanted to kidnap her. Glancing down at her mud-streaked gown, she grimaced. How could he treat her so? Whatever the reason, undoubtedly some kind of desperation drove him. She had seen it clearly in his eyes.

Moving higher still, she peered over a rock and her heart bounced against her ribs. Damnation. Atop his mount, Morgann drove it furiously along the valley path. She ducked down as he scanned the land. What should she do? Continue on? Hide? Though fairly high up, it wouldn't take much climbing to find her.

Endeavouring to put more distance between her and her would-be captor, Alana tied her skirts into a messy knot and kicked off her leather shoes. Climbing was easier without them. The rain slowed to a trickle as she continued her ascent but the ground proved to be sodden and harder than ever to navigate.

Damn the man. What had started as a beautiful morning of freedom had ended up with her covered from head to toe in mud and probably lost in the hills of the Highlands. Dark tortured eyes danced in front of her vision and she cursed him aloud. What had happened to bring about such a change? Was it just her father's treatment of him or was it something more? Ach, well she'd never find out now. She would not stay to find out. How could she when her capture would bring about the worst battle either clan had ever seen? For she knew her disappearance would spark great anger and both sides were just waiting for a reason to slaughter the other.

How she yearned for the days when they stood side by side. It seemed so long ago now yet only eight summers had passed since a time when both families lived and worked together to defeat their common enemies.

She sighed. Dreams of peace were folly, as her da liked to remind her. If they could not return to a time when things were better then all she could do was ensure she did not fall into Morgann's hands again. It was her duty as a Dunleith daughter to keep the peace.

As Alana peered over her shoulder to check on her progress, her footing gave way. She let out a scream as she fell forward, injured wrist giving way as she braced herself. An agonising pain shot through her head and all went dark.

***

The faery's pointed ears pricked up as she heard the scream. Tèile peered at the Highland warrior and waited. He stiffened but continued riding. Silly human. How had he not realised it was Alana? Surely he felt her nearby? But then they had not had much time together yet and he had changed. His heart had become hard and impenetrable whereas Alana's remained open and vulnerable. It was a dangerous combination.

Tèile rubbed a green hand across her face. The stupid horse had spotted her climbing out of the pouch and had been startled. The animal kingdom's ability to see faeries really was a hindrance sometimes. Until she achieved her goal, Tèile was to stay with either Morgann or Alana. She had made the wrong choice, staying with Morgann as he hunted down his ride. She should have realised Alana would never stay, in spite of her burning curiosity. Too dutiful, that girl. But her spirit was to be admired.

She just hoped the girl wasn't grievously harmed. Tèile had little control over the human body, there were other faeries who held that power. The connection between the two humans should have been enough without her having to interfere anyway, what with their shared past, but something prevented them both from seeing what was in front of them.

Jabbing a pointed finger into Morgann's neck as she rested on his shoulder, she chuckled as he scowled and rubbed at the spot. Served him right, foolish man. Did he not know how to treat a lady? Throwing her down into the mud and trying to tie her up was no way to secure a mate. Though Tèile had thought the moment when Morgann had lain across Alana would lead to a kiss and bring her that much closer to goal. She huffed. Silly, silly humans. They were so blind to life.

Eyes closed, Tèile sought out Alana. They were close, she felt her essence calling out to Morgann. She just needed to get him to stop. Mayhap the daft mare could help.

The faery hopped down and clutched at the horse's mane as

she settled herself near its ear and whispered.

***

Casting his gaze around, Morgann tightened his grip on the reins. Foolish lass. Didn't she know how easy it was to get lost in the mountains? Apprehension leached through his limbs and clutched at his chest. If she came to any harm...

Ach, if she came to any harm there would be no one to blame but himself. He should have at least tried to explain or coerce her, not treat her like some prize to be bargained with. But desperation had stolen his manners and his sense. Alana could potentially right all the wrongs of eight years ago and finally bring his stepmother to justice. And he needed to act fast. He could not go on thwarting her plans forever.

Caraid's ears fluttered and Morgann tensed. He couldn't fathom what had come over her. She had never bolted before. *Never.* A sense of something ominous lingered in the air, forcing bile into his throat. Alana was hurt. How he knew that, he couldn't say.

"Hell fire," he exclaimed as his mount's ears twitched again and she skidded to a halt, almost sending him toppling from her.

Gathering his breath for a moment and allowing his pulse to slow, he studied the scenery. He had assumed Alana would take the shortest and easiest route through the mountains but then how well did she even know the land? He'd heard her father kept her locked away and before then she never travelled unaccompanied. Mayhap she had little clue where to go.

And mayhap he'd terrified her that much that she'd ventured up the peaks in an effort to hide from him. God's blood but he was a beast.

Morgann dismounted, swept his wet hair from his face and stared at the peaks on either side of him. It could take days to search each crag and boulder. A prickle swept down his arm and he felt the faint sensation of someone tugging on his shirt. When he glanced at Caraid, she appeared to be motioning with her head toward a point midway up the mountain. He scowled. God's teeth, what was he thinking, relying on strange 'feelings' and the intuition of his horse?

But regardless, he patted her flank. "I'll get her, Caraid. Never fear."

He wasn't sure if he was trying to reassure himself or her. Hand curled around his sword, he began the journey up the mountain, peering around every rock, heart in his throat. Images of Alana fatally injured or worse assaulted him. How could he live with himself if he was responsible for her death?

Unable to prevent himself, a faint smile tugged at this lips as he remembered the sweet lass who'd followed him around since they were young. Their friendship had developed into a firm one of teasing and laughter. But she always took him too seriously, believed too much in every word he said. Mayhap she actually believed he intended to harm her. While he admired her spirit, her naivety always concerned him.

However the years had certainly fed her courage. He couldn't imagine her fighting him off before. Now it seemed she was a determined lass. Unfortunately she was determined to evade him and put herself in mortal danger.

The mountainside proved to be slippery underfoot and he had to snatch out at the protruding rocks to keep his footing as he surveyed the land. A flash of blue fabric snared his attention and he hurried over to it.

Hell fire, Alana's plaid.

At least he was on the right track. But if she was out in the wilds barely clothed, she was bound to catch a chill. The thought pushed him to climb faster until his breathing grew ragged and his limbs began to ache.

And then his heart juddered to a stop.

Morgann clambered up the hillside, dropping to his knees beside her. She lay on her front, caked in mud, face ashen and serene. As he reached out to her, he noted his hands shook. Lord, he'd only just found her again, he couldn't lose her now.

Cannae lose her? She isn't even mine.

Never mind that his heart threatened to burst in agony.

He pressed his fingers to her neck and the agony dissipated

as he felt the faintest of beats. Releasing a long breath, he rolled her tentatively over and used his plaid to wipe the worst of the grime from her face. As he studied the curve of her cheek, he shook his head. Damn everything to hell. This was all his fault.

Too used to keeping secrets, that was his problem. He should have confided in her when he had the chance. The lass he'd known would never have doubted him. But how could he have told her the truth about her father? It would have broken her heart.

One hand under her head, he gathered her into his arms, tamping down on the tremor of pleasure rolling through him. Aye, he did not deny he enjoyed having Alana in his arms but what he would not give to have her in his arms under different circumstances.

Once, all those years ago, mayhap that would have been possible. He'd always clung to the hope that in another life that may have come to pass.

A faint tease of a breath blew across his neck and she mumbled as she buried her head into his neck. He uttered up a prayer of thanks and tried to ignore the shiver it sent through him as he carefully made his way down the mountainside.

Morgann found another decent sized rock once he reached the bottom that would provide enough shelter from the cold. Clicking to Caraid, it pleased him to note the mare's jumpy countenance had calmed and she obeyed him instantly, coming to stand beside him.

Morgann bent down and gingerly pressed Alana under the rock. Lying beside her, he attempted to warm her with his body. Her eyes fluttered open and she grinned sleepily at him as he leaned over to study her head. A tiny dribble of blood seeped from under her hair but it was too wet to tell where she'd hurt it. He prayed it wasn't a deep cut.

"Morgann?" she whispered.

"Aye, 'tis I."

"I am glad ye've come for me." She sighed. "I've missed ye."

He swallowed heavily. God's blood, she must have fallen hard. "I've missed ye too."

She beamed up at him. "It pleases me to hear ye say that."

Delicate fingers began creeping up his arm and hooked over his shoulder, holding him closer. He frowned. "What are ye playing at, lass?"

"Dinnae ye want to keep me warm, Morgann?"

Aye, of course he did. He wished to do more than keep her warm. He hungered to strip her of her clothing and kiss her from head to toe. He wished to plunder her mouth and see if her kisses were like he'd always dreamed they would be. He wished to make her *his.*

But he would not take advantage of her and he needed to remember exactly why he'd taken her. If he handed her back to Laird Dougall ruined, there would be hell to pay. The fates somewhere were playing a cruel trick indeed, placing this wet, sensual woman in his arms.

He huddled up to her, tucking her head into the crook of one arm. The light rain still soaked his back but the discomfort was nothing compared to the agony of having Alana flat against him. Highly aware of her slender legs twining with his, he gritted his teeth and tried to picture something less enticing.

But nothing came. All he thought of was Alana.

She tilted her head up and nuzzled into his neck, breath heating his skin. It sent a shudder through him.

God help him.

As if to torture him further, her lips tickled over his neck and he stiffened, trying to hold her at bay.

"What's wrong, Morgann? Dinnae ye want me?" she whispered against his skin.

"I dinnae want a lass who's had several knocks to the head. Yer brain is addled. Ye dinnae know what ye want."

"Are ye, the brave Highland warrior, afeared of a harmless lass?"

Harmless? He could hardly believe sweet Alana was carefully threading her leg between his and pressing her juncture against his thigh. Her knee brushed against his arousal—aye, he was insanely aroused—and he held back a groan.

"I always thought ye would be the one, ye know?" she

murmured.

He frowned down at her. "What is yer meaning?" Alana's fingers sketched across his collar bone before rasping up across his bristled jaw and he gulped.

"I thought ye'd be the one to claim me."

"Ye mean..." he trailed off, unable to find the words.

"I've never been with a man," she said wistfully. "I always wanted it to be ye."

All the blood in his body threatened to boil over with such words. It was as if the thunderstorm had struck him and his whole body was alive with lightening. Only in scant dreams had he allowed himself to imagine claiming Alana. Their friendship never had the chance to blossom into anything more than just that, but he'd always hoped that one day, when they were older, it would happen.

As had she apparently.

She rocked against him and the world went hazy as her soft flesh rubbed at him through her skirts. Ach, he was certainly being punished. Restraint was not his strong point. Alana's breasts thrust up against him, small and delicate, practically begging for him to palm them.

"Cease, ye daft lass," he forced out as she wrapped her hands around his neck.

"Ye dinnae mean that."

He rolled his eyes as her lips pursed with disappointment.

No doubt she would be furious if he took what she offered when she came to her senses. Where had that sweet lass he'd once known gone? Was it just the knock to her head that had turned her into a sultry seductress or had the years really changed her so?

"Ye wouldnae thank me if I took advantage. Now behave yerself. Ye'll be lucky if ye dinnae catch a chill."

"Ye are no fun anymore, Morgann MacRae." She unclasped her hands from around him.

Relaxing his muscles, he slipped his thigh from between her legs. "Aye, yer probably right." He eased her into the crook of his arm and tried to keep some distance between them. Shivers still wracked her so he couldn't fling her away as he wished to. "Rest some, *m'eudail.* Ye've had too many adventures this morn."

"Yer still planning on kidnapping me?" Her lashes fluttered as she fought a yawn and Morgann's fingers twitched with the need to smooth his palm over her face and soothe her off to sleep.

Funny, because he hadn't felt any such needs in a long time. For too long he had been on edge, striving to protect his father and his lands. War and rivalry dominated his life. That, and anger. Softer sentiments had no place in his life.

He didn't respond. Already her eyes closed and her breathing slowed. Morgann took a moment to study her profile.

Even in rest her chin pointed out stubbornly as her lips parted. They looked soft and tempting. He'd certainly gone too long without a woman, that was it. Feeling lust for the daughter of his enemy, old friend or not, was not good.

Cool. Callous. That's what he needed to be. The fates had landed Alana in his lap for a reason. With her in his clutches, her father, Laird Dougall, would be forced to admit the truth and reveal his plans from eight summers ago. And Morgann would finally have justice and hopefully peace. A tiny noise escaped Alana's lips as she nuzzled into him, her golden curls soft against his neck.

Ach, callous? Holding Alana captive was going to be quite the test of his character.

CHAPTER THREE

A thud echoed in Alana's head as she attempted to pry open her eyes. Someone incessantly pushed at her, pressing her shoulder. Was it her maid? She never normally tried to wake her with so heavy a hand. If she'd only leave her be.

"Too tired," she mumbled as something jostled her again.

"Alana?"

Something rumbled against her back. That definitely did not sound like her maid.

"Ye awake, lass?"

Dragging her eyes open, she winced as her head pounded and sunlight flickered over the horizon. She glanced down. A horse! She was on a horse.

Strong male arms surrounded her, holding her securely and a familiar spicy scent teased at her. *Morgann MacRae.* Of course. It all came back to her. She put a hand to her thumping head. Obviously her attempt at escape had failed and she must have hit her head when she slipped.

"Alana?" His voice mumbled over her hair.

"Aye?"

"Good, yer awake. Ye had me worried for a while."

"Aye, I'm awake." She tried to twist to look at him but straining her neck round hurt her head. "Just. And no thanks to ye."

"I didnae force ye up the mountain," he protested.

She peered around at the scenery through half-closed eyes. The day was growing late. The sun glinted over the hills and cast their tips in an amber glow, drawing out the yellow fauna in the Highlands. Her stomach sank.

MacRae land.

The enemy's territory. What a fool Morgann was. Her father would never let him get away with capturing her. The probable outcome of his rash actions made her stomach churn. Death would no doubt come to both sides. Mayhap even her if the MacRaes wanted.

"I suppose yer still kidnapping me too."

"Aye."

"Yer a fool. Just return me and I'll no' say a word. I swear it."

"Yer in no state to return and as ye said I cannae step foot in Dunleith. Ye'll come to Glencolum and recover while I make negotiations with yer father," he told her coolly.

His tone made her shiver. Something dark and desperate lay

under those words. It reminded her of what she'd seen in his eyes. As if the very devil drove him.

The ache behind her eyes grew worse and she closed them, gave into the urge to rest against his broad chest. Hard muscles prodded into her back but were somehow comforting. Aye, finding comfort in the arms of her captor was not the best of ideas but her head hurt too much for her to think straight.

"The keep is up ahead," Morgann murmured in her ear.

Alana didn't bother to open her eyes. She remembered the keep well from the days when the clans worked closely together. Surrounded by a jagged wall, the main keep towered over the surrounding land, propped up by a tower on each corner. Once, it had been a place she'd be happy to see. Glencolum Keep meant seeing Morgann but now it was enemy territory and who knew what was awaiting her there.

Shadows flickered behind her eyelids and she heard the clatter of a portcullis. Dragging her eyes open once more, she noted the curious expression on the villagers as they passed through the gate. Trepidation tied her stomach tight and forced the pounding in her head to increase. Alana didn't believe Morgann truly meant her harm but no doubt the MacRaes harboured anger over the deaths of their warriors just as her own clan did. The frequent battles and skirmishes between the clans had left many scars.

But the change in Morgann sent a chill through her. She'd

always known he was a capable warrior with a bit of a temper and a rash nature but he'd also been humorous and kind. She only saw the tiniest flickers of such traits in him now. Surely he would not let her come to harm? Even with whatever desperation drove him?

Shudders wracked her and his hold tightened. Ach, but she was weak. The movement of his arms displaced the chill with a great surging warmth. She glanced down at his arm, watched the way the linen pulled tight against his skin as he handled the reins. The slightest hint of a scar peeked out of his sleeve but she couldn't see it properly without pulling back his shirt. Alana knew well how he came by it.

She swallowed and glanced up at the four-storey tower as it loomed over her. Her father's hand had created that scar. Would there be any forgiveness to be had from Morgann or was his anger too deep?

Morgann led his horse over to the stables and dismounted before offering up a hand. Alana wished she could deny his aid but her head still swam and her eyes threatened to bust from their sockets with the thumping.

She clasped his hand, coarse skin warm against hers and risked a glance into his eyes. Pain and confusion echoed in the dark depths and something else... a kind of curiosity. His gaze skimmed over her before she slid from the saddle as he took the time to trace every part of her. Her breathing stilted as she did the same, taking in those powerful legs, wide shoulders and stubbled jawline. His lips twisted into a mocking grin.

For some reason she needed to feel those lips upon hers.

A wild recollection of being pressed against him, her body entwined with his as she revelled in the taut strength of his physique assailed her. Heat soared into her cheeks. Had it been a dream? The memory was disturbingly real. Sweet Mary, her mind really was addled.

A tug on her hand reminded her she was meant to be dismounting and she pushed herself from the saddle only for her feet to go from beneath her. Morgann moved swiftly, hooking an arm around her back and forcing her into him to keep her upright. She latched onto his neck instinctively and found herself bent slightly back, Morgann looming over her.

Which was more threatening? The keep or Morgann?

Morgann, for certain. His dark hair fell over his face, creating shadows in his features as his gaze bore into her. His lips were a scant distance from hers and she felt his breaths gliding over her skin. Her heart threatened to burst from her chest. Did nerves do that or was it something else? If only her captor wasn't so ridiculously beautiful. Morgann was a Highland warrior through and through. Raw, untamed. Like the Highlands themselves.

But no other highlander sent her pulse pounding or forced heat though her body. Mayhap it was just nerves.

Attempting to right herself, the haziness that crowded her mind lingered and she fell flat against him once more. He sighed and scooped her into his arms, and she let out a squeal of protest. With quick strides, he navigated the few steps leading up to the keep and the short wooden bridge creaked and thudded as he carried her across it.

"Morgann, I am no sack of grain. Ye cannae cart me about so."

He ignored her, his hold firm, jaw set tight. She dragged her gaze around as a familiar voice called out a greeting.

Morgann's stepmother, Margot, approached, a slender eyebrow arched as she eyed Alana. Unease pricked across her and she clutched at Morgann's shirt, knowing it was foolish to seek comfort from him but doing it anyway. Margot stalked across the Great Hall, footsteps echoing in the vast space. A fire pit crackled in the middle of the room and massive black chandeliers creaked lightly as a breeze blew through the open shutters of the hall.

"What in the Lord's name are ye doing, Morgann?" the lady demanded as she approached.

Still as unerringly beautiful as Alana remembered, Margot cast cool grey eyes over her, mouth tight. The woman reminded Alana of a raven. Sleek black hair, darker than Morgann's, white skin and refined, noble looks. But those looks hid something sinister, she was sure of it. She'd never seen proof of it but the woman always sent chills through her.

Alana shot Morgann an imploring look. "Morgann, put me down. 'Tis most unbecoming."

"Ach, if I put ye down, ye'll fall down."

"Then put me somewhere safe. 'Tis yer fault."

Margot's eyes narrowed. "Sweet Mary, is that the Dunleith lass?"

Morgann stiffened but kept his hold on Alana. "Aye, this is Alana. She is injured and I have taken her into my care."

Margot crossed her arms across her chest. "What are ye thinking of, bringing the daughter of yer enemy into my keep? She cannae stay."

Feeling ridiculous draped across Morgann's arms, Alana held her chin high, determined to retain even the smallest amount of dignity as she watched their exchange. The undercurrent of aggression on both sides made her wish the ground would swallow her up.

"She can stay and she will stay in *my* keep, and ye'll have naught to say in the matter."

"Yer keep?" Margot asked, a sly smile slipping across her face. "Yer father isnae dead yet."

"Nay, not yet. A disappointment to ye no doubt, *Mother*."

With that he spun on his heels, calling back to her over his shoulder. "Be sure to have some clean garments and a bath sent up."

Shadows swallowed them as he stepped into the stairwell and easily carried her up the winding steps. His lurching movements forced her to hold on tightly and she buried her face against his chest as the dizziness in her head grew stronger.

By the time they reached the top, nausea welled in her stomach. Using a foot to press open the door, Morgann carried her into the chamber. She could hardly bring herself to study her surroundings as he placed her onto a red canopied bed.

He stood over her for a moment, unease etched into his features as he shifted on his feet.

"Ye need not look at me so, Morgann," she grumbled. "I've no intention of dying on ye. Though..." her stomach lurched, "I believe I may be sick."

His eyes went wide and he grabbed a chamber pot and thrust it in front of her as she retched. Awkwardly patting her back, he eased her hair from her face as her stomach emptied its contents into the bowl.

When she had nothing left, he discarded the pot to one side and poured her a drink. Alana took it gratefully, the tang of ale cutting through the taste of bile.

"Ye should never have run from me," he scolded.

"And what did ye expect me to do? Offer myself up to ye?"

He gave a wry laugh. "Nay, I didnae expect that. I didnae expect much of what ye did."

She scowled. Why was he speaking in riddles? The image of her entwined with him on the hills swamped her again. Had that really happened? Was that what he was talking about?

"If yer done pretending to care for my welfare, will ye no' leave me in peace? No doubt yer father will have something to say about my capture. Mayhap he has more sense than ye and will send me home."

"My father will have little to say on the matter. He is unwell. All duties at Glencolum are in my hands so yer pleading will fall on deaf ears."

"Oh." She sagged against the bed. "I didnae know yer father was ill."

His expression twisted into a brief moment of anguish, quickly replaced with a cooler one. "Aye, well 'tis nae something we want our enemies knowing."

"Ye see me as yer enemy?"

He considered her for a moment. "I've never seen ye as my enemy, Alana, but ye are still Dougall's daughter. I'm sorry to involve ye in this, but I have little choice."

Alana pressed a hand to her head, the pounding increasing. "Ye've yet to tell me why ye should wish to bring war to yer doorstep. Ye talk in riddles. I cannae understand ye anymore."

She needed him gone. All this talk of duty and reasons. What reason could he possibly have for capturing her? Was it revenge that drove him? If it was, he was clearly not thinking properly.

"I cannae tell ye why. The less ye know, the better." he muttered. "But just know that if ye were in my position, ye'd do the same."

"How can I know that if ye will tell me naught?"

God's blood but the man was evasive. They used to tell each other everything.

But that man no longer stood before her. Her heart ached for what she'd lost. Shaking away morbid thoughts, she closed her eyes. She heard the grinding of his teeth and assumed he studied her as she lay prone. What did he see? Was he planning his next move or did he reminisce about better days too?

"I'll return to check on ye later."

Waving a hand dismissively as him, she prized open an eye. "Dinnae bother, I need no aid."

She needed to clear her thoughts and figure out how to escape. If she was gone much longer, her father would surely assume the MacRaes had taken her and would be on their doorstep before long, baying for blood. Her father's temper was quicker than Morgann's and he'd not listen to reason.

Morgann studied her for a moment and gave her a brief nod of his head. "As ye will. Behave yerself, Alana. I've no wish to put ye in irons but I will if I have to. Ye've done yerself enough harm for one day."

The callous countenance had slipped back into place, all

HGTV Magazine's cover price is $3.99 an issue and publishes monthly, except Jan/Feb and Jul/Aug combined issues. House Beautiful's cover price is $4.99 an issue and publishes monthly, except Jul/Aug and Dec/Jan combined issues. Both publish monthly, except when combined issues are published that count as two issues as indicated on the issue's cover. Your first issue will arrive in 4-6 weeks. Offer good in U.S. only.

QHRHSTJ7ASWAƎ

BUSINESS REPLY MAIL
FIRST-CLASS MAIL   PERMIT NO. 349   HARLAN IA

POSTAGE WILL BE PAID BY ADDRESSEE

PO BOX 6000
HARLAN IA 51593-3500

NO POSTAGE
NECESSARY
IF MAILED
IN THE
UNITED STATES

Get HGTV and HouseBeautiful for just $18

Save **80%** off the cover prices

HGTV and associated marks and logos are trademarks of Scripps Networks, LLC and are used under license. All Rights Reserved.

OFFER EXPIRES: 03/15/17

☐ **YES!** Send me 1 year of HGTV MAGAZINE and 1 year of House Beautiful for the special price of just $18 total. I save $89.80 off the combined cover prices.

☐ Payment Enclosed ☐ Bill me

Name

Address _____ Apt _____

City _____ State _____ ZIP _____

For faster service: combodeal.hgtvmag.com

Continuous Service Program: Your subscription will continue unless you ask us to stop. Each year you'll receive a reminder notice followed by an invoice for the low renewal rate then in effect. You can cancel at any time at service.hgtvmag.com and receive a refund on all unmailed issues.

concern for her gone and she threw an arm back over her eyes, unable to bear it. The door clunked shut and she heard a bolt slide across. She truly was a prisoner then.

Her empty stomach churned. Rest. That's what she needed. And then she'd work on a plan to escape. Aye, she'd leave Morgann MacRae to his torment. He clearly wanted no help or sympathy from her. Ach, to think of the anguish she'd felt for him all these years after her father's behaviour. That man hardly seemed worth such sorrow.

***

Dragging her hands though her pale green hair, Tèile huffed. Curses, the pair were as stubborn and as confused as each other. She'd sometimes watched them as young friends, waiting for the moment that fate would be fulfilled and their debt would be repaid but as the years had gone by, it became clear interference would be necessary.

Neither had the courage to admit their feelings. Or mayhap they'd been too young to understand them. Humans were very confusing beings. How hard could love really be?

She cast her gaze over Alana as the woman's breathing slowed and she fell asleep. Tèile admired her spirit. The lass was planning some kind of rash escapade but Tèile couldn't allow that. It had been hard enough to persuade Alana to leave the keep and bring Morgann to her. Her interference had to be limited; they had to find their own way to each other.

But there were things she could do. Dreams were an excellent tool of the fae. The *sidhe* council would only allow her so much use of magic. Too much and the mortal world would shift into an imbalance with all the magic in the air. Putting the Campbell clan to sleep for a while had already cost her dearly.

With a wave of her fingers, she grinned as Alana exhaled slowly. She would not need to do much to ensure she dreamt of Morgann. The moment they had shared under the rock had been entirely their own. Tèile had hoped the kiss might happen then but Morgann...

Stubborn human male.

A kiss. That was all that was needed, she was sure of it. Their connection would finally be realised and Tèile could get back to enjoying herself as a faery should. She rubbed her hands together as she thought of the celebrations that would take place. The burden of the *sidhe's* promise would be at an end. Too much faery time had been devoted to the foolish couple. But that was the price they paid for human aid. Many years ago, Alana's mother had helped one of the fae bear a child. Delicate creatures that they were, they occasionally needed a human's aid. And in return they promised to look after Alana. Which meant ensuring she and Morgann married.

Aye, she looked forward to being rid of her tiresome task and indulging in a little tipple or two. Tèile sighed. She would deserve it after trying to get these two to see what was right in front of them.

Silly fools. Couldn't they see they were destined for one another?

***

Swiping a hand over his face, Morgann stormed down the stairs, pushing past a guard at the bottom. His stepmother turned at the sound of his footsteps and placed her goblet of wine on the trestle table at the end of the Great Hall. Swathes of gilded light danced through the rear window, illuminating Margot's curvaceous figure.

He scowled as she slid toward him, a twisted smile upon her lips. A bitter taste sat in his mouth as she skimmed her gaze over him. Too many men had fallen prey to her seductions, his father included, and he didn't doubt she hoped the same for him. But he'd always seen through her stunning looks to the black, ambitious heart that lay beneath.

He would not succumb as easily as his father had.

"Is our guest settled then, Morgann?" she asked as she sidled up beside him.

"Aye, well enough."

"Think ye 'tis wise to bring that lass here? Ye must know ye are inviting war by holding her here."

He clenched his fist, pulling on his self-restraint. For too long, the woman had spread her poison through Glencolum. "I know naught, save that I will do whatever is necessary to ensure the safety of the clan."

"Safety? How shall we be safe under the threat of war?"

"Do ye question me, Margot?" Morgann took a deliberate step toward her.

Her eyes widened briefly before she pulled her shoulders straight. "Nay, of course not. I trust yer judgement."

Morgann seized the moment to study her. She'd acquiesced far too quickly but a flicker of a plot sat behind his stepmother's grey eyes. Turning before she recognised he knew as much, he paced over to the table and poured himself some wine.

"Is my father abed?" he asked without looking at her.

"Aye, my lord husband is sick as ever. But dinnae fear, I have been by his side, faithfully tending to him."

He didn't doubt it. "Well, ye need tend no longer. Have a maid see to him. The keep needs yer attention elsewhere, Mother."

It galled him to call her that. She—only five summers his senior—could never take the place of his mother. But sometimes it worked to put her in her place. While his father lay sick in his bed, he had taken on all the duties of the laird. And thus she was under his command.

But Margot was not easy to command. Slippery and cunning.

Rather like Alana, though she certainly held no wicked thoughts like Margot did.

"Shall I see to our guest? No doubt she is in need of a woman's touch."

He gave her a cold stare over his shoulder. Morgann wouldn't allow his stepmother anywhere near Alana. Surely she knew what he intended to do with Alana and it did not bode well for his stepmother.

"Nay. Ye'll no' step foot in my chambers."

Behind him, Margot huffed and he heard her skirts swish as she stormed away. Ach, now he had two difficult women to deal with. Though he had to confess that he preferred dealing with Alana. A surge of desire burst through him as he recalled the sensation of soft skin and delicate curves pressed into him.

It wouldn't do. Lusting after her would only serve to distract him. Never mind that the warrior in him longed to keep her in his chamber and take full advantage of having her as his prisoner. Not that she seemed to remember the moment she'd thrust that sweet figure up against him.

Lucky lass. That moment would likely torture him for an eternity.

And now she lay in his bed, invading his sheets with her addictive scent.

Morgann squeezed at the stem of his goblet and drew in a breath through his nostrils, hoping to calm the heat spearing through him. The image of the disappointment in her eyes dampened it, a heaviness growing in his chest. He knew he'd changed, that he was no longer the carefree lad she'd known and mayhap cared for. And he understood her need for reasons. But for the moment he had to keep his plans quiet and Alana would find no benefit in learning the truth.

If he could, he would protect her from it to the best of his ability. He wasn't sure how. But he would do that for her at least. Morgann heeded her feelings more than he cared to think about.

With a sigh, he walked over to the writing desk in the corner of the hall and reached for a quill while motioning to one of his clansmen, Kieran. "I need a missive delivering to Laird Dougall Campbell with haste. Stop for naught, ye understand?"

Kieran nodded. "Aye, laird. What shall I say of his daughter?"

"Say naught save what ye must to ensure yer safety. This missive will tell him all he needs to know." Morgann sat and dipped the quill in the ink. "He willnae wish to see his daughter harmed."

CHAPTER FOUR

Night air whispered through the hall, seeping through the closed shutters and Morgann shuddered. He glanced at Margot who sat near the fire pit, carefully embroidering a tapestry. Though she looked engrossed in the task, he knew well enough her mind worked to figure out how to get rid of Alana.

He groaned inwardly. What a mess. By bringing Alana here, he not only risked further fighting but placed her in very real peril. He'd already seen the effects of Margot's plots—his father's health was evidence of that. How she continued her witchcraft on him baffled Morgann. He ensured all food and drink was checked, yet his father still ailed. And he could not accuse her outright of witchery or plotting until he had proof.

Which was where Alana came in.

Margot cared little about war or his clan. She'd been an outsider to begin with until she'd ingratiated herself to his father and climbed into his bed following the death of

Morgann's mother. But she did care about power. And Alana had the power to prove without doubt that Margot was a traitor.

She flicked her gaze up to him and offered a seductive smile. Morgann saw the sinister undertone to it and snapped his gaze away. Aye, if Alana was the key to Margot's undoing then he'd placed her in grave danger.

He sagged into his chair. He'd spent too long watching Margot's every move. It made him edgy. A man was posted on Alana's door and Margot had not been near the kitchens or her room to meddle with Alana's food or bath.

A sharp twist in his stomach stiffened his muscles. So why did he feel as if Alana was in danger this very moment? It was the same sensation that had struck him in the mountains. He jumped to his feet.

"Morgann? Is all well?" Margot asked as several members of the household stared at him.

Ignoring her, he pushed past the men around the fire and took the spiral steps two at a time. Sweat tinged his brow as he reached the top, breaths coming heavily as the sickening sensation grew stronger.

Help her, a voice whispered and he shivered.

Finn, his cousin, and one of his strongest warriors, guarded the door to his chambers and he trailed his gaze over Morgann, brow furrowing. "Laird?"

"Has she been out?"

Finn laughed, crossing both arms across his chest. "Nay, of course not."

"Has she said aught? Begged ye for release mayhap? Made threats?"

"Nay. As quiet as a mouse."

Morgann cursed and shoved Finn aside. "That's what I feared."

Swiftly pulling back the lock, he thrust open the door and stared around. The bed was empty. The wooden bath in front of the fire sat unused. He spun around, half expecting her to leap out from behind the door and make an escape but no one sprang out of the shadows.

Stepping over to the side table, he snatched the only lit candle in the room and lifted it, peering around. His gaze alighted on the bedding tied around one post of the bed.

"God's blood, foolish lass," he murmured to himself.

"She's gone out the window?" Finn asked from behind him. "Brave lass."

Morgann scowled at the admiration in Finn's tone and dropped the candle back on the table. They were four storeys up, almost at the highest point in the keep. Falling would mean certain death.

He stomped over to the window and peered out. He just made out the line of white sheets and what looked like the dark red blankets tied together in a makeshift rope. And then his heart froze.

The faintest feminine voice reached up to him, almost lost in the evening breeze. Morgann listened carefully. Aye, there it was.

Leaning further out, he peered into the gloom and swallowed heavily. "Alana?"

"Morgann? I-I'm stuck."

Halfway down the wall hung Alana, just visible at the end of the line. He just made out the vague outline of her gown and she was clearly nowhere near enough to the ground.

"I-I can't hold on much longer."

The distress in her voice was obvious enough though. It yanked roughly at his chest as urgency rushed through him. He couldn't lose his Alana.

His Alana?

"Finn," he barked, "find a ladder. With haste."

Without waiting for a response, Morgann sprinted down the stairs, almost losing his footing twice, and barged out of the hall doors. A gathering of men stood at the base of the keep, looking up, torches held aloft.

"She's going to fall," said one.

"Aye, she'll no' survive," declared another.

Morgann glanced around. Where in the devil was Finn? Alana screamed and with the torchlight he could now see that she was barely gripping the line of bedding. He had no time. Eyeing the castle wall, he stepped forward and curled his hands over the stone.

"Laird, what are ye doing?" someone asked but he ignored them.

Boots pressed against the keep, he began to climb, fingers barely hooking into the indents between each stone.

"Morgann!" Alana cried.

Pulse quickening, he climbed harder, boots slipping against the rough stone. His fingers ached and he scarcely held on but some wild determination drove him forward. The muscles in his arms burned and he didn't doubt his fingertips would be bleeding by the end.

If he survived the climb that was.

Peering up, he realised he was close. Alana's bare feet dangled not far from his face, flashes of leg peeking from under her skirts. His heart pounded with exertion and horror as her grip slipped and she cried out.

Now she hung from one arm, Morgann knew he had to get to her fast. Disregarding the cramping pain in his hands, he edged up the wall until he was at her side.

She stared at him, eyes wide with fear. "M-Morgann, I cannae hold on."

"Just a wee bit longer, *m'eudail*. I'm here. I'll no' let ye fall."

He reached for the sheets, curled a hand gratefully around

them and gave them a tug. Aye, it would hold his weight. He inched upward and swung over, snatching the line in both hands so that he hung from it just above Alana. Her grasp on the rope slipped and Morgann seized her hand, gripping her tight before she fell.

"Hold on, Alana. I've got ye."

Looking down, Morgann realised just how high up they were. God's blood, his hands hurt. But he kept his hold strong around Alana's.

"Ye cannae hold on to me forever," she exclaimed, voice wavering.

"I dinnae need to hold ye forever," he grunted.

A thud against the wall dragged his attention from her and he blew out a long breath. Finn climbed carefully up the ladder now propped against the castle wall. Morgann's arm shook as he waited for what felt like an eternity for Finn to reach them. The top of the ladder didn't quite reach Alana's feet and Morgann knew he'd have to trust Finn to catch Alana.

Letting go of her was the hardest thing he would ever do.

"Alana, ye need to let go of me. Finn will catch ye."

She glanced down and then back up at him, alarm clear in her gaze. "I'll fall."

"I'll not let that happen. Trust me."

Alana peered down again and nodded slowly. "A-aye. I trust ye."

"Finn?" Morgann called to him. "Are ye ready?"

"Aye, my laird. I'm ready."

Giving Alana a nod, he waited for her grip to loosen. Ensuring she was perfectly lined up with the ladder, he sucked in a breath and let go. Alana screamed as she dropped and Finn hooked an arm around her waist, pinning her to the ladder. They both wavered for a moment but the men at the bottom held the ladder firm.

Morgann almost let go of the sheet as relief made him sag. Jolting, he grabbed the fabric with his other hand and waited until Alana was safely on the ground.

"Laird? What are ye going to do?" Finn shouted.

He glanced up at the window and then at the distance between him and the top of the ladder, he smirked to himself. "Looks like I'm climbing, Finn," he yelled back.

His shoulders wrenched as he hauled himself up the line of sheets but by some miracle he made it to the top and clambered in through the window. Dropping to the floor, he gathered his breath. Sweat dripped from him.

The door to the chamber swung open with a crash and Alana dashed to his side and wrapped an arm around him. "Morgann, thank the Lord yer alive!"

"Aye, no thanks to ye, ye daft lass," he grumbled as he came to his knees and she flung her arms around him.

Morgann allowed himself a moment to savour the press of

her face against the side of his neck and a slight shudder coursed through her. He caressed her hair roughly, reassuring himself she was all right.

Finally finding the strength to come to his feet, he hooked his hands under her arms and hauled her up with him before setting her away.

She clasped her hands in front of her and offered him an apologetic look. "Forgive me, I never meant to put ye in danger."

"Nay, ye just intended to escape. Yer plan was a terrible one, Alana. Yer lucky ye didnae end up dead."

Chin thrusting up, she propped her hands on hips. "'Twas nae terrible. 'Twould have worked had ye given me enough bedding."

"Oh, aye, so 'twas my fault for not providing ample bedding so ye could make yer escape." He swiped a hand across his damp brow, fear slowly replaced with disbelief and anger. Did she not realise how terrified he'd been for her?

"Well…nay, but ye cannae say 'twas a terrible plan. And I wouldnae have had to resort to such things had ye no' brought me here against my will."

Morgann shook his head and began drawing in the sheets. "Ye know, Alana Campbell, I'll be glad when ye are returned to yer father. Yer more hassle than yer worth."

A hurt expression crossed her face as he closed the shutters and dumped the length of bedding on the floor. It shouldn't have bothered him that he'd upset her. She was his prisoner after all. But it did.

Forcing his own expression to harden, he stepped sharply toward her. "No more foolish escapades, ye understand?"

"I'll no' stop trying to escape."

"Then I'll no' leave ye alone."

Actually he liked the notion. He perked at the thought. No more worrying about what she was up to or fearing Margot would get to her. Aye, while he waited for a response from Dougall, he'd be Alana's shadow.

***

Tremors still ran through her body as Alana concentrated on drawing in breaths. Sweet Mary, she'd been close, too close, to death. Ach, if only she'd been more careful and checked how long the sheets were. In desperation, she'd started to descend, unable to see the bottom in the dark. And then she'd become stuck. Without enough strength to climb she had just hung there. *Then* Morgann had scaled the walls.

But he was well. Her desperate attempt at escape had nearly got them both killed but thank the Lord neither of them had fallen. Unfortunately Morgann now looked ready to throw her back out the window. Brow furrowed, muscles flexing, nostrils flaring. Alana suspected she was in grave trouble. Mayhap *she* should fling herself out the window.

Should she fight him? If he remained by her side during her captivity then she would never find another chance to escape and she had little time. Before long, her father would be at the castle walls, threatening war and calling Morgann out.

She skimmed her gaze over the muscles that pulled his linen shirt taut. If her father went up against Morgann death was surely inevitable. And if by some chance of fate her da was victorious, Morgann would be harmed. As much as she didn't wish to be his prisoner, she certainly did not want him dead.

Settling on a softer approach, Alana inched forward and laid a hand tentatively on his forearm. He flinched, the darkness in his eyes increasing.

"Ye dinnae need to do this, Morgann. Release me and we can forget this ever happened."

Morgann snorted. "Ye'd forget me so easily?"

"What is yer meaning? I've never forgotten ye."

"Ye forgot me well enough eight summers ago."

Anger surged up inside her at his petulant tone. Forget him? Never. She'd spent many months worrying for him, wishing things were different. Wishing she had shown some strength and stopped her father.

"I never forgot ye! Never, ye hear me, Morgann MacRae."

Not even when her da accused him of theft and had him dragged away to be branded as a thief. A shudder ran through her as she recalled watching her clansmen haul him to the blacksmiths.

Morgann stared at her, shoulders dropping and Alana saw the fury slowly leave him.

She chewed on her lip, gaze burning into his as she forced herself to speak softly. "I am sorry," she whispered. "I wish... I wish I could have stopped him. Or come after ye." To her dismay her lip wobbled as she dropped her gaze to the floor. "I wish I'd had more courage."

There. She'd said it. For too long, she had longed to see him and apologise. She couldn't help but wonder if she'd begged harder or defended Morgann more vehemently mayhap her father would have let him be.

Morgann stepped forward and tapped a finger to her chin, coaxing her to look at him. "Ye couldnae done a thing, lass. I'd no' have wanted ye to come to harm and my father would surely have used ye as some form of revenge for me."

"Like yer using me now then?" Her lips tilted.

"I dinnae use ye for revenge, *m'eudail.* 'Tis justice I seek." Finger still resting under her chin, he stroked it leisurely down the arch of her neck, sweeping briefly over the pulse point there. "I couldnae use ye. Ye have such courage as I have ever seen."

Her mouth grew dry as his fingertip grazed her skin. The sound of her breaths amplified in her ears as she attempted to keep her voice light. "Ach, ye flatter me, Morgann. But I do regret all that befell ye that day and everything since."

"Everything?"

"Aye, everything. I cannae be glad I am with ye again under such circumstances. Not when ye invite war with yer actions. I've no wish to see ye or my da killed."

"So ye do care for my welfare?" He moved up to trace the line of her jaw.

"Of course I care for ye. Yer my friend. I always cared for ye. I didnae speak to Da for four sennights after what he did to ye!" She grinned at the memory.

Morgann's lips turned reluctantly upwards. "See? Ye have great courage, lass. Yer da is a fearsome man."

Her smile flickered as her heart twinged. "Was. Was a fearsome man," she corrected. "He is aged. Morgann, if ye go up against him, he will surely die."

Morgann dropped his hand from her face and she immediately felt the loss. The desire to snatch and bury her cheek against it was almost overwhelming. How was it a man who used to be no more than a close friend and was now her imprisoner had her so captivated?

"I dinnae want to hurt ye," he told her sincerely. "I feel no affection for yer da but if I can spare ye pain, I will."

"Ye promise?"

"Aye, I'll no' hurt him. But I cannae say the same for the rest of my clan."

Alana nodded slowly. "Ye have my thanks, Morgann. Though I dinnae see why ye have to go to such measures."

"'Tis something I have to do. I cannae explain my motives but 'tis no' for something as petty as revenge, I promise ye."

Shaking her head, she inched closer. "Why cannae ye explain? Ye used to tell me everything, remember?"

"Not everything."

A hand thrust out, he pressed it to her shoulder in an attempt to hold her back. She could hardly think when she got nearer but the heat of his body seemed to suck her in. They were speaking in riddles. Dancing around one another. Both trying to understand what the other wanted. She'd intended to manipulate him, to bargain her freedom. Yet somewhere along the line the past had caught up with her and the burning desire know what had happened those years ago snared her.

And then another kind of desire swept her up.

Alana curled her fingers around his wrist and drew his hand away. She glanced at his arm and paused. Bringing her other hand up, she gently rolled up his sleeve, skimming her fingertips over his skin.

"What did ye not tell me then?"

His throat worked as he swallowed. "I'd hardly tell ye now."

"Ye are a stubborn man, Morgann MacRae." She settled her hand on the scar on his arm, tracing the shape of it—a brand in the shape of a dagger tip. She winced as she considered the pain he must have felt.

Aware her gaze was full of sympathy as she looked back up at him, his flinch didn't surprise her. His jaw clenched again and she saw the anger consume his once more. Would that she could erase it and bring back her friend.

"I am sorry for what happened. The men told me afterwards what they did to ye. My father had no right to punish ye as he did."

Before he could protest, she brought her lips to the scar, dancing them over his skin. He coughed uncomfortably and she savoured the feel of the dark hair on his forearm as it tickled her mouth.

"'Twas no less than a thief and a traitor should expect," he said gruffly.

"Yer no thief and no traitor. I know ye didnae take that ring."

Straightening, he stepped sharply back. She wavered and he tugged her hand from around his arm. Her stomach dropped as his reserve slipped back into place. What had she done wrong? Alana shrank toward the bed. Ach, but she could not understand the man. Here she was apologising and defending him and he behaved as if she had offended him.

He glanced out of the window and sighed. "'Tis late and I am weary after yer escapades. Get into bed. I'll be sleeping on the floor."

Alana eyed the pallet intended for a maid, imagining Morgann's large form sprawled out on it. And then she pictured him elsewhere.

In the bed.

Heat rose in her face. Lord, she couldn't let him stay here. She wouldn't get a moment's rest. For some reason Morgann MacRae made her think all kinds of wanton thoughts. She certainly didn't recall feeling like this during their years growing up together.

Oh aye, she'd wanted to kiss him. Even imagined marrying him. But an ache never developed between her legs whenever she thought of him like now.

As if knowing where her thoughts were leading, he watched her carefully, gaze roaming her body as she curled a hand around the bed post for support.

"Well, are ye getting into bed then, lass?" he asked impatiently.

"I cannae. 'Tis nae proper. I refuse." She forced strength into her voice, determined to find her courage once more. The soft approach was not going to work so she needed to figure out another escape plan.

"Ye'll do as I say. Just because we were once friends, Alana, doesnae mean I willnae force ye to do my bidding. I've been too soft on ye already and look where that lead me. Climbing up the side of my damned keep!"

She huffed. "Well I must relieve myself first and I'll not do that in front of ye. At least take me to the garderobes."

Morgann faltered at this and thrust a hand into his black hair. "Aye, as ye will." Yanking open the door, he motioned for her to step through.

She glanced along the hallway. Should she try and make a run for it? Strong hands snatched her arms and she struggled against his hold, crying out in frustration as he shoved her back into the room and slammed the door firmly shut behind him.

"What are ye doing?" She rubbed her arms where he had grabbed her and saw the flicker of remorse in his gaze.

"Dinnae even think about it," he growled.

"I didnae do anything!"

"Aye, but ye were considering it. Ye'll not escape, Alana. Ye'll leave this castle when I say, no sooner, and ye'd be better off getting used to the idea." He bent and reached for the tied sheets, still curled in a bundle on the floor. "Get on the bed," he commanded.

The tenor to his voice sent a shiver through her. A shiver of fear or excitement? She wasn't entirely sure. Her feelings toward Morgann had become so muddled. She did not want to stay his prisoner yet she hungered to be around him. Aye, those hits to the head truly had confused her.

Still she kept her back straight and maintained eye contact, even as he bore down upon her. "Nay," she said hoarsely.

"On. The. Bed."

"Nay."

With a sigh, he latched his hands around her waist and threw her on the bed. She squealed as the bed ropes creaked and she bounced against the mattress. Before she could push herself up, Morgann was upon her once more, clasping both wrists in one hand as he bound them with the sheets, effectively tying her to the bed.

Eyes wide, she fought uselessly against him. "How am I to relieve myself now?" she asked feebly.

"I doubt ye even needed to but ye'll be able to use the chamber pot with some difficulty."

Alana glanced down. Aye, she'd not really needed it. But she would at some point during the night. Did he expect her to do so with her hands bound and him lying on a mattress at the foot of her bed?

She tugged on her bindings. "And how shall I stay warm now I've got no blankets?"

"Ye should have thought of that before ye decided to use them to escape."

She gave the sheets binding her wrists one last tug, blew her hair from her face and slumped against the pillows.

Morgann smirked with satisfaction and Alana gritted her teeth at his display of male pride. "'Tis bad enough ye've kidnapped me but now ye've tied me up and plan to sleep in my chamber. I'll be ruined by the time yer done with me."

He crossed both arms across his chest and rocked back on his heels as he considered her. "Trust me, lass, if I wanted ye ruined, I had enough opportunity on the mountains."

A knot sat in her throat. What did he mean? Surely she hadn't really—

"Oh, aye." He nodded, making her wonder if she'd spoken aloud or perhaps he just read her that easily. "Ye all but offered yerself to me."

She swallowed the lump, hoping the dim candlelight hid the blush in her cheeks. "I didnae!"

"Said ye'd never been with a man and then threw yerself at me." His teeth flashed. "Yer lucky I'm an honourable man. Many lesser men would have taken everything ye offered and more."

"I took ye for many things, Morgann, but I didnae take ye for a liar."

"I'm no' lying about this and ye know it well. I can tell, Alana. Ye remember that moment just as well as I do." Morgann positioned himself at the end of the bed, arms still folded. He released a cynical laugh. "Many lesser men would take ye now too."

Skin prickling, Alana tried to ignore the thrill his words sent through her as her body remembered the sensation of being draped across that powerful form. In the candlelight, his skin gleamed, along with his eyes. It was no wonder she'd offered herself to him really. Who could resist such a man? She tracked every fragment of him, from the dusting of hair at his collar to the veins in his arms. Unfortunately the end of the bed blocked the rest of him.

"Especially when ye look at them like that."

She snapped her gaze to his face, cursing her obviousness. She never had been any good at hiding her thoughts. "Mayhap ye should take me. I am ruined anyway." She smiled. Oh aye, this could work. Seduce him into letting her go. Not that she'd ever seduced a man before. In truth, she'd never even kissed one.

Eyes hooded, Morgann's gaze followed the line of her skirts—where she knew her ankles were on display—up to her breasts, and lingered on her face. Each part of her singed, as if he had touched her rather than just looked. The faint buffet of the wind against the shutters drowned out the sound of her own heavy breaths but it failed to cover the pounding beat in her ears. How long he studied her, she couldn't be sure, but if felt like forever.

And then he spoke and it was not long enough.

"Ye make a tempting offer but I'm in no habit of taking lasses against their will."

"Why would it be against my will?" Embarrassment flamed through her as she heard the desperation in her voice.

Sweet Mary, was it all part of the plan or did she truly long for him to make her his? What she had told him in the mountains had been true. Long ago she'd believed they would probably marry and he would be the one to take her maidenhood but never like this. And she never expected to yearn for it so badly.

He moved unexpectedly around the bed and dropped down beside her. Palms pressed into the pillow, his arms framed her, chest flat against hers. Her nipples peaked against him at the feel of hard male flesh and his hair tickled her cheek as it fell across her face. A hint of fruity wine lingered in his warm breaths and she blinked as his lips came to her ear. Her hands came up to press him away but somehow ended up fastened to his chest. A heavy pulse against her palm echoed the one in her chest. She shuddered as his breath fanned over her skin.

Firm lips danced over her chin and his tongue darted out to lick at the corner of her mouth. A tingle bolted through her and she forgot to breathe. She went rigid. *This isnae how a first kiss should be!*

"Ye dinnae know what ye want, Alana," he whispered. Thrusting himself away, he stood and shook his head. "And I'll no' fall prey to some wild plan ye've hatched to get under my skin."

"Do I?" she forced out of a tight throat.

"Do ye what?"

"Get under yer skin?"

His jaw twitched and he backed away from the bed. "I'll no' play these games anymore, lass. Ye'll stay here, unharmed, and be returned in exactly the same condition as ye arrived in. *Once yer father has agreed to my terms.*"

"Which are?"

Morgann lowered himself into the carved oak chair by the fire and began unlacing his boots. Alana watched his nimble fingers with fascination. What would they feel like on her bare skin? She pressed her lips together. Lord, had she wanted him to kiss her after all?

He glanced up at her. "Ye need not know. If all goes to plan, ye'll be safely installed back in yer keep before long, none the wiser."

Alana blew out a frustrated breath. All these secrets. It was so unlike Morgann. Hadn't they once shared everything? With a four year age gap, they'd become good friends as soon as Alana was able to walk. Morgann's mother loved to tell of how Morgann doted on her even as a babe. How had things gone so wrong?

She observed him as he strolled around the bed, his walk confident and sure. If only she felt so assured. That deep intent gaze latched on to hers briefly as he leaned over and blew out the candle.

"Sleep now, lass," she heard him say softly.

Had she imagined the longing tone to his voice?

CHAPTER FIVE

With a grimace, Morgann stretched his aching arms. Ach, sleeping on a straw pallet was nothing like sleeping on a feather bed. His bed. The bed that Alana occupied. Scraping a hand through his hair, he pushed to sitting and peered at the bed. Only bare feet peeked out over the edge, small and pink. A strange urge to wrap his hands around them and warm them struck. He glanced over at the fire, noting it died during the night. It was likely Alana was cold. Remorse assailed him.

He clambered to his feet and extended his arms, barely covering a groan as his muscles protested. It was her fault. He followed the line of sheets and sighed as he took in the sight of bound wrists. She slept on one side, hair splayed across the pillow, mouth slightly ajar. Her chest moved with each deep inhalation, the gentle curves teasing him with their smoothness. Hand rasping across his jaw, he took a step closer and let his gaze linger on her parted lips.

In sleep, she looked so innocent. He smiled to himself. But innocent she was not. A temptress in disguise that one. Though mayhap she did not realise quite how tempting she was. Her rash words last night had very nearly broken through his self-control. He could never do it and live with himself, but the primitive part of him ached to take her and make her his.

She moaned quietly and tossed, and he leaped back, only relaxing when she remained asleep. He studied her once more. Was it just her beauty that enticed him? Alana had always been a pretty lass, though he'd not paid much attention to it. Only after he'd been banished did he begin to regret that they would never reach the point of marriage, something everyone, including them, assumed would happen.

Her spirit was to be respected to be sure. Though he could do without it right now. What was to be a simple kidnapping was becoming quite the trial. But he saw something of himself in her. That determination and admirable loyalty to her clan. He understood that. Mayhap that was why the pull to her was so strong.

Shaking his head at himself, he backed away, slipped on both boots and walked to the door, careful to open and close it quietly. If she had slept as badly as he, she needed rest. He paused outside to lace his boots and listened. Would she attempt another escape? He didn't think she was foolish enough to try and scale the wall again. He straightened and bolted the door, running a hand through his hair again in an effort to tidy it. A wash and clean clothes had to wait until he found someone to mind Alana.

Morgann nodded a greeting to his men as he strode across the top floor and followed the spiral stairs to the hall. Most of the men were gathered for breakfast, occupying the two long tables that had been set up for the morning meal. Shouting and the clatter of knives filled the large hall and Morgann grinned at the sight. Many good men sat at his father's tables. He would surely do everything in his power to protect them.

His gaze settled on Margot, sat at the top table, her lady-in-waiting at her side. He narrowed his eyes as they conversed, heads together. Neither of them could be trusted. While he did all he could to watch her and keep her from his father's side, she was still the laird's wife and there was a limit to his power. Somehow she ensured his father stayed bedridden.

His closest friend, Finn, told him he was foolish to blame his father's ill health on Margot but he knew it was her.

Knowing eyes connected with his and a sly smile skimmed across Margot's lips.

Without a doubt, the woman wanted his father dead. If he had succeeded all those years ago, he would have had solid proof. As it was, none believed him, not even his father. But his father was so blinded by her beauty and seductive ways.

Aware he was glowering, he stomped across the hall, briefly patting a hand to Finn's shoulder as he sat at the end of the table.

Finn dipped his head in greeting and grinned. "Good morrow, laird."

"Good morrow."

"Sleep well?"

Morgann rolled his eyes as he caught the lewd edge to Finn's grin. "Aye, well enough," he replied curtly.

"And how is our guest?" Margot leaned over, drink in hand as she pressed her breast into his arm.

"I know not."

"And how could that be? Ye slept in her chambers all night did ye not?" She smiled seductively. "Or mayhap ye did little sleeping?"

Morgann tried to shift away but she moved closer, thigh brushing his through her gown. "I was there to ensure she didnae attempt an escape, naught more."

"Are ye expecting me to believe ye spent the night with a pretty lass and did naught? Or mayhap she rejected ye?" Margot laughed lightly.

"Rejected ye?" Finn interrupted. "Surely not. Morgann has never been rejected by a lass!"

"Naught happened," Morgann said firmly as he snatched a chunk of bread from the platter in front of him.

"Well," Margot declared, eyeing him over the edge of her wine cup, "no one will believe it. Ye might as well have taken yer pleasure for she's all but ruined now."

"Naught happened," he repeated through clenched teeth. "And anyone caught saying otherwise will have me to deal with." He glared at Margot and she backed away, sniffing dismissively.

Morgann turned his attention to his meal though he had little appetite. He satisfied himself with a long drink of ale. Being sat next to Margot often stole his appetite but he suspected it was another woman who robbed him of it this day. Draining his cup, he swiped his mouth with the back of a hand and caught Finn studying him.

"Ye want something?"

Finn chuckled. "Nay, laird, naught."

"Then cease staring at me like some lovesick lassie."

The smile on his friend's face expanded at this. "I dinnae think I'm the one behaving like a lovesick lassie."

Morgann groaned inwardly. If Finn recognised his idiotic behaviour then mayhap everyone else had too. Though Finn knew him better than anyone.

Instead of confronting him, knowing full well that Finn took great delight in riling him, he came to his feet, bending to address him briefly. "I've to see to my duties. Will ye check in on our guest? I dinnae trust her and, in the light of day, she may try something else." He turned and paused, a hand to Finn's shoulder. "And dinnae let Margot near her," he murmured.

Finn rolled his eyes and nodded. "Aye, of course. I'll no' let the little lass get the better of me, never ye fear."

Morgann ignored the veiled insult, well used to Finn's antics. "Aye. Good day to ye then. I'll come check on our guest shortly."

Pushing past the servants clearing away the food, Morgann stepped out of the arched doorway and stood on the bridge that connected the courtyard to the castle. He sucked in a long breath and studied the clear skies with a frown.

An odd storm indeed, the one that caught them both unawares. Almost as if the fates intended for them to be stuck out in the hills. Shaking away the foolish notion, he marched across the bridge and took the stairs up to the ramparts, two at a time. A fresh breeze blew over the top of the wall bringing a sense of promise.

Something was to change. He could feel it. Hopefully his missive would be in Laird Dougall's hands before long and he now had no choice but to admit the truth to his father. Finally Glencolum would be free of the witch's conniving schemes and his clan truly safe.

***

Alana moaned as Morgann wrapped his thick hands around

her wrists, pinning them down as he assaulted her mouth again. Mindlessly she rocked her body up into him, the warmth of his mouth drowning out everything. Only heat and hardness and heavy breathing existed.

She opened her eyes and a blanket of red greeted her. She scowled and tried to tug her hands free from Morgann's grip but he refused to release her. As her tired eyes cleared, she realised Morgann had gone. And she wasn't in her bed at home. Alana struggled to rub the sleep from her eyes but something yanked on her wrists.

Glancing down, she spied the sheets tied around her hands and groaned. A dream. It had all been a dream. And the unfamiliar red fabric was the canopy of Morgann's bed. At least she assumed it was his bed. She'd never been in these chambers before but a masculine scent lingered on the sheets.

She remained a prisoner of Morgann MacRae.

Sweet Mary, but that dream had been vivid. She blew her tangled hair from her face, hoping to cool her skin a little. Ach, dreaming of her captor was no good thing. She needed to remain detached if she was to find a way out. And she had very little time. With only a day's ride between the castles, her father could well be on his way now. Though she imagined he would want to gather his men first.

Footsteps sounded outside her door and came to a stop. She bolted upright and attempted to comb back her hair from her face with bound hands. Her heart sank as Finn stepped into the room, a huge smile on his face.

"Good morrow, my lady."

Alana raised a brow and went to fold her arms over her chest, only for her bindings to prevent her from doing so. "Ye need not play the chivalrous nobleman with me, Finn. I know ye are as discourteous as they come."

"Ach, Alana, ye wound me." He gave her an injured look.

She studied the fair giant of a man, trying to resist the twitching of her lips. He'd changed little over the years, still tall and broad with long hair and a slightly bent nose. Not that it marred his strong features. Men like Finn took pride in their battle wounds and women seemed to admire them just as much. He was indeed handsome, so how was it Finn didn't inspire imaginings like Morgann did?

"Are ye going to behave yerself now, lass?" He stepped forward and drew a hand from behind his back, revealing a bundle of clothing. "I have a clean gown and plaid for ye. Thought ye might need them after yer adventures yester eve seeing as ye never had a chance to change."

Taken aback by his thoughtfulness, Alana opened her mouth and clamped it shut. Finn always had been tender hearted, even when she'd known him as a boy. Why couldn't she hunger after him instead of the inconsiderate, brutish laird?

"Aye, well, I thank ye," she muttered and, realising how

petulant she sounded, she offered a reluctant smile. "'Tis thoughtful of ye."

Finn placed the garments into her hands and sat on the end of the bed. "If I release ye, ye'll no' try to escape will ye?"

Alana glanced at the slightly ajar door then at Finn and finally at her wrists. She couldn't see herself getting very far past the large warrior. Mayhap she could appeal to his soft side once she was dressed. And she longed to remove her grimy gown. It had been soaked and caked in mud and dragged against the stone of the castle. No wonder her bit to seduce Morgann had failed.

"Aye, I'll no' attempt anything."

Nodding with satisfaction, Finn placed her wrists in his lap and began tugging apart the sheets. "God's blood, Morgann really didnae want ye escaping, did he?" he exclaimed as he battled with the knot.

"I think I made it tighter when I tried to wriggle out of them."

Cursing, Finn brought the bonds to his mouth, using his teeth to pry the knots apart.

Alana jumped as the door swung back suddenly, thudding on its hinges, and Morgann stepped in, his expression dark. "What the devil is going on here?"

Finn dropped her wrists. "Just seeing to the lass, my laird."

Alana gulped but Finn showed no sign of nervousness at

Morgann's ferocious expression. Instead, his smile widened.

"Get out!" Morgann barked. "I'll see to her."

"Ye willnae!" Alana exclaimed, a tremor of apprehension making her limbs weak.

She did not want to be left alone with Morgann, not when he looked ready to tear her, or mayhap Finn, apart. And certainly not after that all too real dream. Would she even be able to look at his mouth without picturing it on hers?

Finn patted her hands and removed them carefully from his lap. "All will be well, lass. Will it not, laird?"

Morgann's scowl deepened, eyes blazing. "'Twill be once ye get back to yer duties."

Hands held up in surrender, Finn chuckled and came to his feet. "Aye, aye, I'll be gone. Though ye'll remember ye told me to watch over her."

Arms folded across his chest, Morgann glowered. "Well I'm here now so yer relieved. And I didnae tell ye to bloody undress her."

"I wasnae undressing her. But I can see there's no arguing with ye, Morgann." Finn dipped his head briefly to Alana. "Good day to ye, lass."

Finn closed the door carefully behind him and Alana watched Morgann warily. Strange how the daggered look he sent her caused a tumult of sensations, stretching from fear to excitement. Dark hair grazed his eyes as he narrowed them, lips pulled into a grim smile. Part of her longed to reach out to him, pull him down and remove that expression. And the only way she could think of doing that was by kissing him. The need burned through her as she studied his mouth.

But her hands were bound. A blessing, mayhap, for she could ill afford to fall foul of these ridiculous thoughts. The steady throb of desire seemed to hum between them, barely disguised by the anger simmering off his being. What had she done wrong?

"H-have ye sent word to my da?" she forced out.

"Aye. No doubt we'll be hearing from him soon."

"When he's at yer walls, threatening war, ye mean?"

Morgann gave a decisive shake of his head. "He'll no' be threatening war, ye just wait and see, lass."

"I dinnae know how ye can be so confident. Ye will have angered him and my da has a temper."

He distractedly curled a hand around his forearm, covering the spot where the scar was. "Aye, I know."

"So what do ye intend to do with me in the meantime?" The pressure around her wrist was slowly turning her hands tingly and she *really* needed to relieve herself.

His expression changed. The anger making his body stiff slowly gave way. She noted the softening of his shoulders but it was the change in his eyes that captured her attention. Once dark with annoyance, a carnality resounded in them as he let his gaze settle on her lips.

She opened them, trying to suck in enough heated air to clear her confused mind. It was as if he knew what she'd been dreaming. And her own gaze did the same, lingering on his firm lips as they pulled into the faintest hint of a smile. Was he considering what other things he may do with her just as she was with him? The fire behind her thoughts should have frightened her but there was something instinctual and primitive behind them, as if it was always intended for her to feel this way about Morgann.

The discomfort in her body nagged at her once more and she wriggled and coughed, effectively breaking the moment. Morgann raised his gaze to her eyes and crossed his arms, the warrior slipping back into place.

"I havenae decided what to do with ye, yet," he told her coolly. "I doubt very much I can trust ye to behave."

"Well ye need to at least release me. There's little I can do now."

He studied her silently for a moment and Alana fought the need to squirm under his frank appraisal. "I think mayhap I should keep ye here until yer da comes for ye. 'Tis nae often I have my enemy's daughter tied up in my chambers."

"Ye cannae keep me tied up! How will I... relieve myself?"

Morgann laughed. "I'll no' fall for that one again!"

"I've been tied up all night! Ye must at least let me use the garderobes. Yer enemy's daughter I may be, but I am still a lady. Ye cannae expect me to remain like this." His countenance remained taciturn and unyielding and Alana's hope dwindled away. How did one argue with a man so callous? "Ye never used to be so cold hearted, Morgann," she added softly. The man she once knew still existed, surely? Mayhap she could appeal to him.

"All right," he muttered. "I'll take ye to the garderobes but yer hands will stay bound. I'll no' have ye making a fool of me again."

"But how shall I change?" *Or relieve myself?* Her cheeks warmed. She wasn't sure how to handle her skirts with hands still tied.

He shrugged as he strolled over to the bedpost and began to untie the sheets. "I care not."

"Ach, ye'll care when ye hand me over still caked in filth and Da calls ye out."

"Mayhap I should help dress ye then." A wicked glint illuminated his gaze as he fisted the sheets in his hand and came to stand before her. With a slight tug, he had her on her feet, using the bedding tied around her wrist like a leash.

Alana frowned, chest tight. The endless sides to Morgann MacRae baffled her. The faintest hint of the playful lad she'd known lay under that deadly gleam but it was smothered by more intense emotions.

"Ye tease me?"

"Mayhap." He gave a little yank and she stumbled forward, smacking into his chest.

Before she could react, rough fingers pressed under her hair, teasing across the skin of her neck, down to the top of the lacing on her gown. He gave the ribbon the lightest of tugs, making her breath hitch.

"Morgann, pray cease," she managed to whisper.

He froze, cursing quietly as he took a step back. With a wry laugh, he tapped a finger under her chin—the gesture returning her to a time when they had nothing to worry about. He always used to do that to her. Whenever she took life too seriously, whenever she got over-emotional. It was his way of drawing her out of it. Was she taking *him* too seriously? Was it some twisted game?

"Will ye promise not to get yerself into any more trouble if I release ye?"

"Aye, I promise." An easy promise to make. She had little intention of getting into trouble. Next time she tried to escape, she'd do it properly and make no mistakes.

"Ye'll no' get anywhere if ye try anything. The walls are well guarded."

Alana nodded. That she well knew. If she'd even made it down the side of the keep, she hadn't figured out how to get past the watchmen. She'd have to bide her time and hope an opportunity presented itself though she had little time. War was almost certainly imminent.

***

Tèile watched Alana through narrowed eyes from her spot on the windowsill. She swung her slender legs playfully, long skirts swishing. The girl was planning something again. If only there was more she could do. Unfortunately Alana seemed to have a nose for trouble and if she wanted to put herself in dangerous situations, there was little to be done.

If only they would act upon their attraction. She crossed her arms over her chest and huffed as Alana offered up her wrists to Morgann to be untied. Like Finn, Morgann struggled to undo them and had to use his teeth. Alana's face blossomed with colour. The pull between them was so strong Tèile could smell it. She simply didn't understand. What was so hard about giving into one another?

Still she'd bought them a little more time. Morgann's messenger, Kieran, was right now having a wonderful time with the nymphs. Having lured him in, they were no doubt helping him to indulge in all kinds of carnal delights. No man could resist the tree folk. She propped her chin on a hand and blew out a long breath. At least *he* was having fun. If these two didn't hurry up, she was likely to die of boredom.

***

A hand clasped around her wrist, Morgann led Alana to the garderobes.

"Ye need not hold onto me, Morgann," she protested from behind. "I already said I'd not get into trouble."

Aye, she had. But he still wasn't sure he could trust her. Something about the look in her eyes, that faint glimmer of hope, told him she wasn't finished creating turmoil.

Never mind that she caused such turmoil in him. Her smooth skin against his palm made his gut clench. He tried to wipe the way she stared at him when he'd taken the knots of her bindings in between his teeth from his mind. Those wide eyes and short breaths lingered in his memory.

Had he scared her or was it something else that caused such a reaction? He had frightened her with his anger but she seemed to bounce back from it, ready to lash out with her tongue once more. The thought that, maybe, just maybe, she felt the same burning temptation as he did both terrified and thrilled him. The need to act on their attraction increased.

Releasing her wrist, he remained silent as she brushed past him and closed the door to the garderobes, flicking the briefest of glances his way. He flattened his forehead against the wood and groaned. Just a few days more, he reminded himself. A few days and she'd be back with her father and he would finally be able to relax. With Margot banished or in irons, Glencolum would no longer be at risk. And nor would Alana.

At the moment it seemed the biggest risk to her was him.

The door swung open abruptly and he jolted upright. Hands clasped in front of her, Alana perfected a meek, submissive pose, eyes pleading and bright.

Ach, but it worked. He, the great warrior, felt his knees weaken. It took all his willpower not to drop to the floor and beg to do anything for her. A MacRae bought to his knees by a woman. Well, he wouldn't be the first. Margot had already done the same to his father.

"Morgann," She smiled sweetly, "I thank ye for releasing me. Is there any chance of having a bath sent up? I have need of a wash."

He tensed his jaw. As if he needed the image of Alana bathing in his head. Unable to stop himself, he studied the sweep of her neck, imagined water dripping down it. The thought forced a lump into his throat.

Realising she awaited an answer, he cursed inwardly. "Ye had yer chance yester eve. I cannae spare anyone to tend to ye now. And readying a bath takes too long."

Alana scowled and took a step past him. Morgann wrapped a hand around her arm, holding her in place. "Where do ye go to, lass?"

"If ye'll not send for a bath, then I'll go do it myself. In case ye hadnae noticed, I'm filthy."

Her words forced him to skim his gaze over her gown. Her

adventures had left mud smears on her clothing and face. Unable to stop himself, he reached out and skimmed a thumb across the grimy mark on her forehead.

"Aye, I can see that," he said gruffly, watching the slight flutter of her throat as she swallowed. The memory of the gentle warmth of her skin under his thumb remained and he clenched his fist. "Ye'll have to content yerself with a quick wash. Finn already brought ye some clean garments."

"He always was thoughtful," she said softly.

A faint bubble of anger burst inside him and he struggled to tamp it down. Would he ever forget the image of Alana with her hands on Finn's lap or Finn's mouth practically touching her skin? He loved Finn as a brother but, by God, the thought of him being in Alana's affections tore at his gut.

"But I cannae do my hair myself." Hands going to her hips, she dragged him out of his thoughts. "Ye must have a maid to spare."

Morgann pinched the bridge of his nose and spun on his heel, forcing Alana to scurry along behind him.

"Well?" she persisted as he pushed open the door to his chamber and ushered her in.

"I've no maid to spare. The keep takes time enough to manage." Thanks to Margot's negligence, he thought bitterly, the castle was barely running properly. He spent half his days making up for her idleness, ensuring the servants and soldiers knew their duties.

Alana released a grin, a spark of amusement reaching her eyes and his insides near crumpled. What in God's name had her so amused?

"Ye'll just have to do it then," she announced as she sauntered over to the washbowl propped on a tall oak side table and snatched the linen towel that rested beside it.

Eyeing him, she loosened the ribbon barely holding her braid in place. Hair spilled over her shoulders, thick and luxurious in spite of the streaks of stone dust that still marred it. His fingers twitched as his stomach roiled and he blinked.

He let out a light laugh. "Ye cannae want me to do it."

"I do."

Throat clogged, he shook his head. Was she attempting to seduce him once more? She had little idea how close she'd been to succeeding when she'd all but offered herself to him the previous night. It would have been so easy to strip her gown from her, to stroke every womanly fragment of her until she begged him to take her. And she would. If she felt as he did, there would be no denying him. But Alana, sweet Alana, deserved so much more than that. He could never treat her like that. Bad enough that he had to take her prisoner.

She flung the towel at him and he fumbled to grab it, brow creasing as she leaned over the bowl, the ends of her hair dangled into the cool water.

"Ach, ye cannae expect me to do women's work," he tried in desperation.

Alana tilted her head sideways, gaze latching onto his as streams of hair fell across her face. One eyebrow rose. "I didnae take ye for a coward, Morgann."

Damnation. He sucked a long breath in through his nostrils and stepped sharply forward. He saw the faint flicker of triumph on her face before she turned her head over the bowl. He snatched at the jug resting near the washbowl and pressed his free hand against the exposed skin at the back of her neck. *Pale. Fragile.* His hand looked too strong, too rough next to her flesh. A sharp awareness of the power he had over her rushed through him, the primal need to conquer and command fresh in his mind. What was it about Alana that made him feel more a warrior than when he spilled blood on the battlefield? And yet, she was the one conquering him. She already had him doing maid's work. It was an odd balance of power they had. While he commanded the physical side, she commanded the emotional one, toying with him with great skill. Grudgingly, he admired it. He wondered if women did not have the upper hand sometimes. Strength only got you so far.

Water trickled over her as he tipped the jug and Alana gasped. The water was cool and it made her shudder. It reminded him of the last time he'd seen her wet and cold, when she'd been tucked against him in the middle of the mountains.

Hot, scalding lust assailed him. With a smirk he debated throwing the chilly contents of the jug over his head instead, though he doubted it would have much effect.

Angry with himself for letting lust get the better of him yet again, he thrust his fingers into her hair, massaging the water roughly through her tresses and she yelped.

"Morgann, gentle!"

He shook his head. Was he really doing this? He allowed his touch to soften, scrubbing as he imagined a woman would. Ach, if anyone caught him doing this...

The texture of silky hair under his fingers soon erased his discomfort. Alana's hands clutched the edge of the table, knuckles white. Did she enjoy his hands upon her? Oh, he'd rather have them elsewhere, but he had to admit, there was something soothing about doing such a menial task for a woman. Nay, for *Alana*. To know he was looking after her provided an odd sort of comfort. Morgann sighed. If anyone deserved looking after, it was Alana. A shame it would never be him, not after the truth was revealed. Her father would never let him near her again.

"T-there's some tonic, I think. A-a maid brought it up yesterday."

Her voice sounded thick and strained, echoing the tension in his throat. Throwing a glance around, he spied the bottle on the bedside table and took both hands from her hair to reach for it.

Alana remained bent over the bowl, bottom thrust out, the curve of it clear against her skirts. He took just a moment to enjoy the sight, even as he cursed his lack of willpower before pulling the stopper from the bottle and giving it a sniff. It smelled of flowers, soft and feminine like Alana and another, undesirable scent lingered beneath it. He shrugged and tipped some of the oil-like substance into his hand.

"How much—?"

"Just a little."

Ach. He eyed the pool of tonic in his palm and tried to tip some back into the bottle. When he thought he had enough, he pressed his fingers to either side of her head and raised it away from the bowl, allowing him to smooth the oil into her hair. Alana sighed as he worked at her scalp. What he would not give to do the same to the rest of her.

Alana. Naked. Covered in oil. Sighing as he trailed his fingers over her slippery skin.

Hell fire.

One restorative breath later, he'd finished and almost had control of his senses. Offering the towel, he forced himself to turn away as she used it to dab at her wet hair. The chambers were too small, the air too stifling. He had to get out. A glance over his shoulder held him in place as she eyed him.

Water dripped down her face and lips, her hair a tangled mess over one shoulder as she continued to rub the towel over it. The years disappeared and he remembered the girl who had once been his best friend. And yet that girl wasn't nearly as enticing as the one stood before him. Both of them combined were a potent mixture.

"Thank ye," she said with a gentle smile.

Mayhap just one moment wouldn't hurt. Just enough to remove her from his thoughts. A strange weakening sensation invaded his muscles and he turned to take the towel from her unresisting hands. Throwing it over her shoulders, he used it to draw her toward him

"What are ye doing, Morgann?" she asked breathily, cheeks darkening.

A heavy pulse resounded through his head as he patted at her hair. "Taking care of ye."

Lips parting, she dropped her gaze from him, golden lashes fanning against her skin. "Ye dinnae need to do that."

"I like taking care of ye." Inwardly he groaned. Where had that come from?

"Ye take care of many people." That green gaze latched back onto his, making his chest tight. "I see that, ye know? I remember the pride ye took in yer clan, in being the future laird."

"Aye, well..." Hell, she read him far too easily. It should have terrified him but it didn't.

"I like ye taking care of me." The colour in her face spread and her pulse fluttered beneath his thumb.

He groaned as he moved closer still. "Ye create a weakness in me, Alana. It makes me wish—nay *long*—for things to be different. A highlander should never be weak." His voice came out raw and ragged.

She moved up onto her tiptoes, closing the gap between them. Her lips were temptingly close and he watched them carefully as she spoke. "There's no weakness in knowing what ye want."

"I dinnae think ye know what ye want. Unless ye are hoping to seduce me into letting ye go again."

Alana pressed her lips together, supressing a grin. "Ye've already said I cannae seduce ye. Did ye lie?"

"Mayhap."

Warm breath skimmed his lips. Was she seducing him or was he the one playing the game of seduction? She lured him in yet made no further moves. The final decision was his.

He surrendered. What other choice did he have? With a growl, he claimed her mouth, the heat of her lips making his stomach flip, his skin prickle. Grip strong on the towel, he kept her pinned to him, almost afraid she would make an escape.

And while he anticipated his reaction to her, he didn't expect her fiery response. Moist, gentle warmth greeted him as she opened her mouth and flicked her tongue over his bottom lip. His entire being tensed. She widened her mouth with a small whimper, allowing him better access as her hands trailed up his arms and around his neck.

Damp hair snagged briefly in his stubble as Morgann tilted his head to get to the sweet taste of Alana. Better than the finest wine, her flavour was subtle and wholly addictive. In the back of his mind, he feared he may harm her tender skin with his rough bristle but nothing would prevent him from making the most of this kiss.

The floral scent of her hair seemed to increase with the heat of their kiss. Little murmurs and soft, sensual sounds came from Alana as he twined his tongue with hers, greedily taking all she could give. His grip around the towel remained firm, not quite trusting himself to let his hands explore her figure. Somewhere, deep down, he remembered he only intended to kiss her.

Even though his body screamed for more.

Nails dug into his neck as she squirmed against him, breasts prodding into his chest. He tasted her once more, a deep lingering kiss before drawing back. It near killed him but somehow he managed to place a second, more chaste kiss on the corner of her lips and relinquish his grip on the towel.

She sighed—in disappointment?—as he broke the connection. He was still close enough to see the bloom in her cheeks dissipate, to view the glossy succulence of her mouth. How wrong he'd been. One kiss would never be enough.

Rubbing the back of his neck, he retreated a pace. A simple movement, but it made his chest ache and his body cool rapidly. Alana offered a little half-smile of understanding. The woman really did know how to read him.

"Will ye be locking me up again?" she asked suddenly.

Well if she'd intended to soften him toward her, she'd succeeded. "Nay, if ye swear ye'll no' put yerself in harm's way again, ye can have free roam of the keep."

"I thank ye, Morgann. I'll no' get into trouble, I swear it."

He was going to regret this. He tightened his grip on the back of his neck before releasing it. "I've duties to see to. Will ye manage yer gown on yer own?"

"Aye, of course."

"Good. Fine. Well... good day to ye, Alana." Morgann dropped his head into a formal bow and twisted away before he changed his mind.

He smacked a palm against the cool stone after he pulled the door shut behind him, the sharp sting doing little to discharge his frustration. *One kiss.* What a fool. He only hoped Laird Dougall would be on his doorstep soon. How much longer he could resist Alana was anyone's guess.

***

Alana dropped heavily onto the bed. How she had even remained standing when Morgann had broken off the kiss she didn't know but somehow she'd managed it. Fingertips to her lips, she stared, unseeing, out of the window.

Sweet Mary, what a kiss. Her *first* kiss. Were all kisses like that? She'd been toying with fire when she'd begged him to wash her hair. Something about having a rough highlander playing maid had amused her and he deserved some hardship after everything he had done, but she hadn't realised quite where it would go. If she said it was all part of a game, a way of bargaining for more freedom, would that lessen the memory of the kiss?

But it was no game. Not for either of them. Her naïve idea of seduction never ran as deep as that kiss had. Morgann's mouth on hers, his tongue exploring every part of her, now etched into her mind. And in her heart...?

Indeed, Morgann MacRae had probably captured a little bit of that too.

She ran her fingers through her damp hair, sighed and got to her feet. The cold touch of water against her skin as she cleaned the remnants of her adventures from her arms and face did little to dampen the heat lingering in her body. Yet again, she wished things were different. If only her father had never accused Morgann of theft. If only she'd been braver and gone to his defence. Emotions battled within. Morgann capturing her could only lead to more heartache and strife but if he hadn't, she never would have discovered that the friendship between them had blossomed into attraction. An attraction so strong she barely comprehended it.

But attraction was not enough. The lad she'd known had to lie somewhere beneath that rough exterior. He revealed glimpses but mayhap he was buried too deep. With her father—and clan—in danger, giving into a desire that held little promise was pointless.

Alana dressed quickly, the chill of the wind through the open window against her damp hair making her shiver. She might as well make the most of the little freedom she'd been granted. Mayhap she would find a way out. Aye, she'd promised she'd not get into trouble but she never made any promises about not escaping.

Briskly tying her hair into a braid, she tossed it over her shoulder and straightened her red plaid. Hopefully Morgann was too busy with his duties and she'd not have to face him quite yet but she was hungry. She slipped on a pair of leather slippers that had been left for her. They were slightly too large but would do her well enough.

Concluding she was a ready as she'd ever be, she pressed open the door and peered around. No guard awaited her, no one demanded to know what she was doing, so she slipped out and made her way down to the hall.

The morning meal was long over, the tables cleared away and Alana patted her empty stomach with sympathy as it growled. Most of the men were likely seeing to their duties and only a few servants lingered in the hall, sweeping the rushes and wiping down the long tables.

Margot lounged in one corner, spread across a bench, some embroidery hanging limply from one hand as she rested an arm across her eyes. Alana frowned. Did she not have anything that needed seeing to? Having effectively taken on her mother's role since the age of thirteen, Alana knew how much work running a keep took. And with her husband sick, Margot should have been at his side.

Alana took a tentative step forward and Margot lifted her arm, eyeing her from under it. "So yer no longer a prisoner?"

"I am no longer confined to my chambers, at least."

"Morgann's chambers, ye mean." Margot moved sinuously to her feet and strolled over to the main table. Pouring some wine, she eyed Alana over the brim as she took a sip. "He didnae harm ye did he?"

Unease settled in Alana's chest. She doubted Margot cared for her welfare so what game was the woman playing? "Nay, of course not."

Chin up, Alana stepped over to the table and helped herself to an empty goblet, copying Margot's movements and taking a large gulp of wine.

Margot smirked. "Ye are lucky then. Morgann is not the man he used to be, Alana. Ye'd do well to avoid angering him. I dinnae know what he was thinking bringing ye here."

"Morgann wouldnae harm me, he swore it."

"Ye have not noticed a change in him?"

Alana shifted her feet, glancing down briefly. Of course she'd noticed a change in him. He carried around a great weight on those vast shoulders. Whether it was his father's illness or the constant fighting that caused the deep furrows in his brow and the jaded look in his eyes, she didn't know, but she didn't like what Margot implied. Morgann was no liar and the man who had been her friend was still there, just hidden.

"Aye, he is changed. Indeed he has grown much since I saw him last." Alana grinned. "In fact I think he may be a whole head taller."

Eyes narrow, Margot dropped her goblet, wine sloshing over the rim as it clunked on the table. "Ach, yer a fool. He'll only use ye. Ye must make yer escape while ye can." She edged toward her. "Ye are in grave danger. He is bitter and jealous and it eats at him."

"I already attempted an escape. 'Twas none to successful."

"Aye," Margot's lips twisted, "'twas a sight to be seen. But ye must try harder."

"Why do ye care anyway? Should ye not be supporting yer laird in his decisions?"

"He is not my laird!" she spat. "My husband is my laird. Morgann will never be laird."

Alana took a step back, the venomous tone taking her by surprise. Why would Morgann never be laird? What did she mean? She wasn't sure she wanted to know. Anger and something sinister darkened Margot's eyes, forcing Alana to hold the questions on her tongue.

"Trust me," Margot continued when Alana failed to respond, "ye dinnae want to make the mistake of trusting Morgann. Jealously will drive a man to much desperation."

"What does he have to be jealous of?"

Pausing to secure her gaze on her, a smile slid across Margot's face. "Me."

"Ye?"

"Aye. He loved me ye see. Wanted me for himself. And then I married his father. He's not been the same since. Why he's even accused me of witchcraft."

Alana blinked. Morgann loved Margot? Surely he would have confided in her when they were friends? A sharp twisting pain stabbed at her heart. But he'd said there was something he never told her. Could that have been it? And witchcraft? It was hardly an accusation to take lightly. Morgann surely knew that saying such a thing might see Margot burned. While Alana didn't trust the woman, she'd never stoop to accusing even her worst enemy of witchcraft. Morgann had to be driven by something very grave indeed. Or... mayhap wild jealousy provoked him.

Alana twisted away and blindly sought the arched doorway. When she stepped outside, she scanned the walls for any sign of Morgann but he was nowhere. The man was so reticent, it was enough to drive her mad. If she confronted him about Margot, would he even admit as much? She barely managed to get two words of explanation from him as it was. Only that this wasn't about revenge. She sorely hoped it wasn't. The thought of him caring for that woman made her hands curl into fists.

Well, if he wanted to be so shady then let him. She threw up her chin and strutted down the steps. For she had better things to think on. Like how she was going to escape his clutches for good.

CHAPTER SIX

The air in his father's chambers smelled sour. Morgann eyed the shrivelled old man surrounded by pillows and blankets and sighed. Hard to believe his father had once been a great leader, bringing about peace and many victories for the MacRaes. Ranald MacRae was respected far and wide.

Floorboards squeaked as he stepped carefully across the room, candle flames flickering as he brushed by, and his father awoke. It took a moment for him to focus on Morgann and he grinned in recognition.

"Morgann, lad, 'tis good to see ye. Is all well?"

Morgann resisted the need to wince at his father's scratchy voice and how he greeted him as if he hadn't seen him in days. Which was likely true. He avoided seeing his father, using his duties as an excuse. The sight of his father so decrepit tore at him, made his gut clench with despair.

He concealed his discomfort with a grin as he came to his

father's side and dragged the small wooden chair closer. "Good morrow, father," he greeted as he sat. "Are ye well?"

"Aye, aye, well enough. Have ye seen Margot this morn? I've not seen her yet."

"She's busy, Father."

"She is? What have ye got my bride doing? For surely I cannae persuade her to take her duties seriously."

Morgann let slip a wry smile. "None can, but I try."

"And here ye take yers too seriously."

"Someone has to."

"I worry for ye, lad. Ye cannae bear everything on those shoulders of yers. Ye need to share yer burdens."

"With someone like Margot ye mean?"

His father gave a gruff laugh. "Margot is well enough for an old man like me but ye need a woman like yer mother. One of good character."

In spite of himself, Morgann laughed, trying to ignore the voice at the back of his mind that told him he'd already found one. "Ye mean she's good only for a quick tumble. Then why did ye marry the woman? Father, there's more to that woman than good looks. She has a black heart."

The old man shook his head. "She's just a simple lass. Ye need to realise that, Morgann. Not many women are like yer mother, so I settled for what I could get. She keeps me warm as long as I keep her in fine clothes and that will do for me. Soon ye'll find yerself a good lassie of strong character and Margot will be content not to have to worry about her duties."

Morgann fought the urge to grimace. They'd debated Margot's character many times and the man refused to believe she was anything but a beautiful, empty-headed woman. But Margot was not so simple. If she was, Morgann would have little to worry about.

"So have ye any news for me?"

Pressing his fingers to his temples, Morgann debated telling him of Alana's presence. In truth, he didn't know what to say and he feared making his father sicker, but he also needed him to know of Margot's plot. He'd wondered if Margot intended to make his father aware of Alana's captivity but decided it was unlikely. If Alana disappeared suddenly, Margot would have no one to answer to but himself and would still have the protection of being his father's wife.

With a sigh, he forced a smile across his face. "Nay, Father, no news. All is well."

***

Alana saw little of Morgann that day or the next two. It riled her for she urgently wanted to confront him. And kiss him. She shook her head. Nay, not kiss him. Anything but that. If what Margot had told her was true then sharing another kiss with him was more senseless than ever. She certainly didn't want to be some other woman's replacement. And who could compete with such beauty?

She slumped onto one of the chairs that sat around the edge of the hall and glanced at Morgann's stepmother who was clearly inebriated. The woman drank a lot. Alana plucked at the fabric in her hand and yawned. She was in no mood for embroidery. Her feet twitched with the need to do *something.* There was still no word from her father. Morgann had even sent another messenger out that morning. Why was he delayed? Was he gathering an army strong enough to knock down the walls of Glencolum? Her stomach twisted. She hoped not. A siege would bring such devastation to both sides she hardly dared to think on it.

And she'd still found no way out. Margot had hinted at her being able to escape through a drainage gate in the wall but mayhap Morgann had thought of that as there was always a guard posted in front of it. She blew out a breath. It was hopeless.

The large hall door swung open, letting in a gust of cool air. The day had begun grey and cloudy, gradually turning into heavy rain, leaving Alana feeling more like a prisoner than ever. Morgann strode in, his dark hair damp and spikey. Water dripped down him and moulded his plaid to his body. Alana knew she was gaping as she watched his every move but couldn't look away. The linen of his shirt was almost transparent, revealing every indent in his physique. He rubbed a hand over his face and glanced at her.

Alana yelped as she jabbed her needle into her finger. Cheeks heating furiously, she looked down to see blood pooling on the pad of her finger. The sight made her stomach roll which was odd for she normally had a strong stomach. As she brought the finger to her lip, she lifted her head and gulped.

"What have ye done to yerself, lass?" Morgann demanded as he came over and snatched her hand.

"Naught." She tried to drag her hand from him but he kept his grip firm as he inspected the damage.

He blotted the finger using the sleeve of his shirt and gave her a tilted smile. "Daft lass," he said softly.

Had she imagined the affection in his tone? He certainly didn't sound like he was scolding her. Mayhap she'd mollified him with her good behaviour. A faint spark of hope alighted in her chest. Mayhap he'd be more willing to talk about releasing her. Or at least explain his reasoning's.

"Ye've been gone all day," she said hoarsely.

"Aye."

"Yer duties have kept ye busy?"

He pulled the linen away and checked her finger. "Aye."

"Morgann—" Her voice shrivelled up as he brought her hand to his lips and briefly kissed her knuckles.

"All better." He released her hand and she rubbed at where

his lips had touched.

Damn the man. How could he confuse her so? One minute he was kissing her, then ignoring her, and then being the most chivalrous man she'd ever met. She coughed as she peeked over at Margot who watched them closely and remembered that she wanted to speak with him.

"Morgann, I must speak with ye. 'Tis... 'tis about..." she dropped her voice, "Margot."

Morgann's eyes flashed briefly at the mention of his stepmother. "What has she done? Has she harmed ye? Threatened ye? Curses, I—"

"Nay, nay, nothing like that." She frowned as she studied his reaction. Surely he wouldn't think such things of Margot if he loved her?

"Come with me then," he commanded suddenly, offering a hand.

Alana took it, a faint sensation of dizziness coming over her as she stood. She blinked. While his touch usually incited many sensations, it never normally made her nauseous.

Morgann led her out into the archway of the door. The wind and rain buffeted but the stone protected them from the worst of it. And Morgann positioned himself so that he shielded her from the rest.

"Ye could have taken me to yer chambers."

"I cannae be in yer chambers, Alana. 'Tis no' a good idea."

"After that kiss ye mean?" She couldn't believe she'd said that aloud. Her mind was muddled and she wavered slightly as bile rose in her throat. Sweet Mary but she did feel queer.

She saw Morgann's brow furrow in the light of the torches on either side of the door. "Alana, is all well? Ye look a little pale. Do ye need something? Is that why ye needed to speak with me?"

"Nay..." A strange foggy sensation had reached her ears and her voice seemed muffled. She put a hand to the wall for support as her legs tingled. Something was not right. She threw a desperate glance up at Morgann, praying he would understand as her knees threatened to buckle. Sweat blossomed on her forehead and she leaned back into the castle and closed her eyes. The world swayed beneath her and she just heard a shout of dismay as the wall stopped supporting her.

***

With a giggle, Tèile dunked her head into the wine, slurping at the fruity liquid. Not bad. She swiped a hand across her mouth and grinned. Not like fae wine but very nice indeed. She sighed as the pleasing sensation of slowly loosening limbs pervaded. Taking one last glug, she slumped against the goblet and eyed the stepmother. What a vile woman. Even the faeries who liked to play tricks on humans were more pleasant. A deep seated evil lingered in that woman, one that could not be explained. An inbred nastiness, Tèile concluded.

She shook her head and peered out the door at Alana's silhouette. What was the lass doing? Kissing him hopefully. She rubbed at her temples. How had the kiss not worked? She had been so sure that but one kiss be would be all it would take. Anyone could see they were meant to be together. Even Margot, manipulative woman that she was. She dare not risk Alana getting close to Morgann in case he told her the truth and she actually believed him. In fact, Morgann's stepmother wanted Alana gone. Yet more for Tèile to worry about.

What a mess.

Alana wavered sideways and the faery rolled her eyes. The lass surely knew better than to be affected by Margot's lies. Both Morgann and Alana's hearts screamed for one another. How she could ever doubt him, Tèile didn't know.

Though the foolish man did hide much from her. Somehow she needed to get them to open up to each other. A feat easier said than done. Tèile looked longingly at the wine and then at Alana and released a slow breath. This job was going to take much longer than she expected

She tottered as she stood and fluttered her wings experimentally. Aye, she'd fly in a straight line enough. It was not like she had much distance to fly. She scowled as Alana shifted out of her vision, a sense of unease trickling through her.

With a flutter of her wings, she flew unsteadily across the hall, resisting the urge to give Margot a sharp poke or play a trick on her. She wasn't meant to let Alana out of her sight.

As she sailed out of the door, she adjusted her wings to combat the slight breeze and pivoted around to the spot where Alana had disappeared from her view.

Oh by the stars.

***

That pain stabbed at Morgann and he watched in horror as her feet gave way and she slid sideways down the wall, her skirts catching on the rough stone as she slipped. At the last moment, he dropped to his knees and hooked a hand under her head, barely preventing her from hitting the ground. She crumpled completely, hands limp by her side, eyes shut. Nausea burned his throat as he tucked her into his hold and studied her ashen complexion. Already pale skin looked deathly white and as he followed the line of her throat, he realised her breaths were shallow. Too shallow.

"Hell's teeth!" he shouted.

Finn and several other men had gathered around and Morgann glanced over at his friend. "Where is that damned witch?" Rage made his voice shake. "Get me Margot."

"Morgann..." Finn placed a hand to his shoulder.

Morgann shucked the hand away and stood, cradling Alana carefully. "Just get her," he pressed through his teeth.

"Aye, laird. But ye cannae accuse her of witchery. Alana may just be suffering from a malady."

Swallowing unsteadily, Morgann skimmed his gaze over her still features. "'Tis no malady. 'Tis poison. I know it."

With a sigh, Finn stepped aside to let him past. "I'll send for the healer."

Morgann didn't even acknowledge his words. He was too intent on getting Alana to his room. Servants stared as he carried her in through the hall but Margot was nowhere to be seen. He bit back a snarl of frustration. Damnation, this was all his fault. He had been aware he was putting Alana in danger by bringing her here. She was the one person who could reveal Margot for what she was and there was no way Margot would allow her to be used to force the truth from Laird Dougall's lips.

Kicking the door to his chambers open, he eased her onto the bed. She made no sound, her breaths barely audible even when he placed his ear near her lips. He brushed a finger down her nose and lips, soft flesh now cool. Ach, to think he'd been kissing those beautiful lips not long ago and they had been so full of heat and life. What he would not give to have her awake, shouting at him for capturing her, demanding to be released.

He sat beside her and twined his fingers with her limp ones.

Morgann brought the back of her hand to his mouth and his chest ached as he skimmed his mouth over her clammy skin. He almost expected her eyes to spring open and for her to smack him around the face for kissing her but she remained motionless.

"Alana," he tried, his voice scratchy. "Wake up, *m'eudail*. Pray, wake up." His eyes felt hot and he clenched a fist. Damn that Margot to hell. And damn him for not taking steps to protect Alana. If she died...

If she died it changed everything. If she lived it changed everything too.

The realisation of how important she was to him flooded through him, making his heart thud erratically. Alana had always been part of his life and even in the eight years they'd been separated, she remained in his thoughts. Seeing her once more... Well, the attraction was undeniably powerful. But he also realised how much he missed that lass he'd shared everything with.

Almost everything.

He never told her that he expected to marry her one day.

A hard knot formed in his throat as he swept his lips over her hand again and again. How could he let her go again? If he returned her to her father, he would never see her again.

If she lived.

"Forgive me, *m'eudail*, I shouldnae have been so blind. Yer more important than revenge. More important than the clan even. Wake up so I dinnae have to let ye go."

The door creaked but Morgann couldn't drag his gaze away from Alana. Heavy footsteps came up behind him.

"Margot's gone."

Jaw tight, Morgann swivelled his head around, fixing his glare on Finn. "Ach, damn that witch to hell."

"If she wasn't guilty, then she's certainly made herself look it."

"She poisoned Alana, Finn. I know it. She couldnae afford for the truth to come out and Father would never believe me without proof. Alana was supposed to bring me that proof. I should never have put her in danger."

"Ye did what ye needed to do."

"I should have found another way. Should have gone against my father and had Margot banished anyway."

"If Margot has done everything ye say she's done, then she'll no' be driven away so easily."

"I dinnae know all Margot's plans but she's determined to see my father and the clan destroyed."

Finn sighed and glanced over at Alana, scrubbing a hand across his chin. "The healer is on her way. She's gathering up some herbs. I'll start the search for Margot. She cannae have got far."

Morgann turned his attention to Alana as Finn retreated, the door closing with a soft thud behind him. Only the faintest movement of her chest reassured him she was still alive. For how much longer though?

"Forgive me, Alana," he whispered gruffly, squeezing her hand between both of his. "I swear I'll do all I can to make this right if ye just wake up."

He didn't know what he would do. He barely cared. The thoughts that had driven him ever since he'd discovered Margot's plot to kill his father and take their lands had all but left him. Rage had been replaced by desperation and devastation, leaving him weak, so very unlike a warrior. If Alana died he doubted he'd continue to be much of a man. Already she had him reduced to a begging fool, urging a dying woman back from the brink. If only he lay there instead, the poison working its deadly magic on him. Alana was not meant for such an end. Nay, she was meant to spend the rest of her days finding ways to aggravate him surely?

The rest of her days? Aye. If Alana awoke, he wasn't sure he could let her go. But would she even have him? Somehow he would make a deal with her father and make Margot pay. If he could convince Laird Dougall that Margot intended to harm his daughter, he would have nothing to do with her. He needed to make sure his stepmother paid for what she'd done to Alana. Ach, but he'd been so close to telling her all. Debating whether she could handle the truth anyway. But if his father didn't believe him, why would Alana? And if she did, she'd realise how callous her father was.

He clenched his eyes shut and offered up a prayer. Alana had to wake. She had to. And he would cease being a fool and tell her just how vital she was to him. Soon enough he would have her vibrant and argumentative in his arms once more, revelling in her heated lips and silken skin. Aye, she would return to him.

A cold fist of dread clenched at his heart. She had to for he didn't know how he would continue on if she didn't.

Watching carefully, he willed her to open her eyes but the only response that greeted him was the slowing of her breaths, the faint rasps of Alana trying to cling to life. His throat ached in desperation as he battled his emotions, the realisation that she may never awaken thrusting through him, as sharp and as powerful as the steel of a sword.

Alana was dying and there was nothing he could do about it.

CHAPTER SEVEN

Thrusting a tiny finger into Alana's chest, Tèile sighed and slumped onto the front of her gown. All was lost. The poison Margot put in that hair tonic was very powerful. Death awaited Alana as surely as a faery loved to drink. It had to be that evil woman that had done it. There was no poison in the wine. Tèile drank enough of it to know that but one sniff of the hair tonic and she knew it was hemlock.

Morgann hadn't noticed yet but his hands were red from the potion. Lucky for him, his hands were rough and coarse and he'd only touched the liquid briefly. Alana had spent several days with it slowly seeping into her skin. As soon as Tèile got the chance, she'd ensured the tonic disappeared.

Head in her hands, she released a wry laugh. Finally Morgann understood his feelings for Alana. What was it about humans that meant it usually took a disaster for them to see what was right in front of them?

If only she hadn't indulged in the wine. She should have been watching Alana more closely. From now on, she was never going to drink again. Or maybe only drink a glass every now and then. A glass a day perhaps. Now death awaited Alana and the *sidhe* council would not be happy. Tèile would probably be banished. No more parties and balls. It was enough to make a faery cry.

The rasps in Alana's chest told her the inevitable was just around the corner. A vow would go unfulfilled and the fighting between the clans promised to continue. Many men's deaths would sit on Tèile's shoulders.

She fingered one of Alana's golden locks as the rise and fall of her chest beneath her began to slow. She glanced up at the Highland warrior, devastation etched into his face. He knew as well as she did that Alana wouldn't come back from this. Tèile wracked her mind. Surely there was something she could do? If a faery could not save a human life every now and then, what was the point in being a sacred being? Nodding slowly to herself, she fluttered her wings, allowing them to lift her away from Alana. She stopped briefly by Morgann and pressed a gentle kiss to the man's cheek. He didn't feel it but she hoped he sensed the comfort she tried to offer. With one last look at the couple, she flew out of the window, a barely muffled roar of anguish making her shudder as she slipped into the night.

***

The silver goblet smashed against the wall with a clatter but the sound brought him little pleasure. He stumbled to pick it up and debated throwing it again but it would do little to calm his anger. Placing it on top of the wall, he stared out into the dark, lit only by a few torches dotted along the walls. Clouds filled the sky, blocking out the starlight and Morgann felt a grim satisfaction at the sight. A night like this shouldn't be beautiful. Nay, this night he wanted the clouds as grey and as depressing as he felt.

High up on the ramparts, the wind buffeted at him. It left him chilled enough to almost dampen the warmth of the copious amount of mead he'd drunk. Silence surrounded him. Thank the Lord. Sympathetic looks and words of concern made his stomach churn. They had no idea how he felt. Hell, he'd only just discovered exactly how important Alana was to him. And he could do without their fears on his shoulders right now. Laird Dougall's wrath hardly concerned him. He'd offer himself up if needs be. Finn could take his place easily enough.

He dug his nails into the top of the stone wall as he stared down the length of the keep into the bailey. With Margot gone, he had no one to offer to the laird for punishment. That woman surely had the ear of the devil to have escaped them. She must have realised Morgann would never let her get away with poisoning Alana. It was a rash and foolish move on his stepmother's behalf. He ought to be relieved she was gone but until his stepmother was brought to justice, he wouldn't be happy. And the thought of her still out there... he doubted he'd seen the last of her.

Sucking in a long breath, he swallowed down the lump in his throat and sketched a finger over the cold stone. He and Alana came up here in more peaceful times and talked endlessly. His lips slanted into a wry grin. In the years since, he'd forgotten how to talk to people. He used to share almost everything with her. The one thing he had never told her was how he felt about her. At the time he considered it to be a strong affection but mayhap it had been love. Either way, he knew he would marry her someday. If only he'd taken the time to tell her. Who knew if she had even felt the same but he was certain she felt *something* for him.

He scuffed the ground with his boot, kicking up a loose stone. It was too late now.

Morgann swung the jug hanging from one hand up to his lips and took drink, frowning when only the smallest amount of sweet mead slid down his throat. Surely he'd not drunk the whole jugful? Ach, now he would have to go the kitchens and get some more. He twisted around, put a hand to the wall as the world tilted slightly.

Heart leaping into his throat, Morgann froze. The jug dropped from his fingers and the pottery smashed against the stone floor. He scrubbed a hand across his face and blinked, trying to shove aside his drunken haze. Good Lord, how much had he drunk?

He stumbled forward, arm outstretched. Was he going to be haunted by her for the rest of his days?

"Morgann?"

His knees threatened to buckle beneath him. "God's blood," he whispered. She had to be an illusion, but it didn't stop him from closing the gap and bundling her into his hold. He held her head between both hands and pressed a fervent kiss to her forehead. "Alana?" he muttered as his shifted his lips desperately down, seeking her mouth. "'Tis ye?"

"Aye," she mumbled before he took her mouth in a frantic kiss.

She was warm and soft and alive. Surely she was alive? A ghost should not feel so good. A sound of anguish bubbled in his throat as her tongue met his and he failed to hold it back. Was she truly alive? The pain of losing her still sat in his chest. The memory of her last breath still rang in his ears. How could it be?

Unwilling to release her for fear it was all some dream, he tangled his fingers into her hair. Mayhap he tugged too hard as she whimpered but he couldn't control the frantic movements of his hands as he clasped her to him, seeking a deep, firm kiss.

Feminine hands came around his back and worked under his shirt. Soft fingers stroked his skin, making his entire body tingle. He longed to do the same to her. Only disbelief prevented him from throwing her onto the ground and stripping her bare to repay the favour. He had to know she was real.

Hauling his mouth away, he dragged his lips across her cheek and buried his face in the crook of her neck. She smelled so vibrant, so alive. What in God's name had happened?

"Yer alive, aren't ye?" he muttered into her hair.

Alana laughed and withdrew her hands from his shirt, stroking them up and down his arms. "Aye, I'm alive. What is yer meaning, Morgann?"

He pulled back to look at her, seeing her scowl in the torchlight. By God, she was beautiful. That sweet chin remained thrust out as ever. Even in confusion, her eyes were enough to bring a man to his knees. And those lips... Puffy from his kisses, he knew in better light they would be red and rosy.

"Do ye remember naught?"

"I—" Her scowl deepened. "I swooned, did I not? It doesnae surprise me. I'd not eaten in a while."

"Alana, ye—" he gulped, "—ye died. Poisoned. I was there by yer side. I saw ye breathe yer last breath."

"Poisoned? Dinnae be daft. I know I swooned. I even remember... I remember ye talking. But I couldnae open my eyes for some reason."

"Did... did ye hear everything?"

A smile played on the corner of her lips. "I think so. I remember ye begging me to wake up. I tried but I couldn't. Ye sounded worried. Ye said," her smile expanded, "ye didnae want to let me go."

Morgann groaned and rubbed a thumb over her cheek. "I didnae think ye could hear me. But I dinnae understand. Ye died, lass."

Alana raised a brow at him. "I think ye've been indulging too much, Morgann. Yer wits are addled."

"The healer confirmed it. Finn saw ye. Ye were dead!"

Her smile slipped at his tone and her gaze locked onto his, searching his eyes. "Yer serious aren't ye?"

"Aye, I lost ye, Alana. I thought I'd never have ye back in my arms again."

She softened into him. "Morgann, we need to talk."

"Aye, we do."

"Margot—"

"That witch willnae be able to hurt ye. I'll protect ye, I swear it. We need to leave Glencolum for a bit. 'Tis no' safe here."

She forced herself back in his hold. "Ye believe Margot poisoned me? Morgann, this is just silly. Ye cannae be accusing—"

"Ye dinnae believe me?" He dropped his hands from around her and stepped back. Of all people, he was sure Alana would believe him. After all, she'd been the only one to defend him when he was accused of theft.

"I'm no' saying that, it's just... ye must see 'tis a tall tale indeed. Poisoned, dead, brought back to life. I think I'd know if I'd been poisoned!"

Despair drenched him. Even the person who knew him the best didn't believe him. Teeth gritted, he widened his stance in an attempt to wrestle back some control. He'd already proved himself weak around Alana. He dare not allow his need for her to cloud his judgement and put her at risk again. In his gut, he knew Margot wasn't finished with them. Desperation clearly drove her now, or else she would never have stooped so low. Mayhap she'd hoped to pass it off as an illness and indeed, they'd found no proof of poisoning. But Margot's disappearance only served to prove her guilt.

"Ye could just return me to my da. I'll be in no danger there," she tried tentatively.

He took a step back and raked a hand through his hair. "I'll no' return ye. Yer staying where I can be sure yer safe. And I cannae step foot on yer father's lands."

Alana crossed both arms over her chest as her eyes flared. "Yer overreacting, Morgann. Even if 'twas poison, I'm in no danger now. Give me a mount and let me go and I'll tell my da 'twas all a mistake."

Morgann gritted his teeth and stepped forward again, snatching an arm. "What part of 'I'll no' let ye go', do ye not understand? If yer on yer father's lands, I cannae protect ye."

She wiggled in his hold. "Morgann, yer as pig-headed as ever. When will ye learn ye cannae command me?"

He released her slowly. How had they gone from kissing to arguing again? Things were meant to be different now. The relief he'd felt as seeing her once more, at the miracle of having her back in his arms, had been replaced with pure frustration.

Aware his anger may get the better of him, he turned and stalked away, stepping into the stairwell. He paused briefly to view her through the arch. "I'm taking ye to the Old Castle. Ye have no choice in this, Alana. Ye may have little care for yer safety but I'll no' go through losing ye again."

Without giving her a chance to respond, he stormed down the steps in search of Finn. Now he needed to make preparations. And have yet another messenger sent out. Morgann paused briefly on the stairs and cursed aloud, the harsh words echoing off the stone. Hadn't he sworn to do things differently? To be honest and open with her? And all he'd succeeded in doing was angering her and frustrating himself.

He needed to get her to safety. That had to be his priority. Once he did that, then he would concentrate on being a better man. Mayhap if he proved himself to be honourable, she would trust his word. It was not as if he'd given her much reason to hold any trust in him. Kidnapping her, near ravishing her, tying her up. Aye, he'd done little to prove himself. From now on he would be the perfect gentleman. Morgann released a snort. Well, he would try his best at least.

***

Chin thrust out, Alana huffed as Morgann directed the mount through the valley. She struggled to cling on to her annoyance as Morgann's chest rubbed against her back, his hold strong around her as if she were a precious cargo. Yet again she was being treated as if she were some prize. Nay, not a prize, a *tool.* Something with which to win wars. She tried to summon more anger but it fizzled inside her. The way he looked at her after she fell ill... and held her so tightly. As if she truly were something precious. For a brief moment, everything changed. They were a man and a woman again and there was no war or plotting or secrets. But he closed over once more. She was beginning to doubt Morgann could ever let go of the past and be the lad she used to know.

His legs chafed hers and she fidgeted in the saddle. Not that the man was entirely unappealing. The determination and focus he displayed was something she never saw in him before. Potentially Morgann MacRae was the most amazing man she'd ever met. If only she could see but a bit of how he was before.

Alana stared at the horizon as she drew in deliberately long breaths. She looked forward to seeing the Old Castle again but knowing she'd be in such close quarters with Morgann for who knew how long made her skin prickle and her mind reel. Why hadn't her father come for her yet? Even if he hadn't received the message, he surely must have figured out what had happened. With the tension between the two clans as strong as ever, his first assumption would be that the MacRaes took her.

And now Morgann was taking her away. Finn would negotiate with her father and send him onto them, as long as he brought no army. This much she'd at least managed to get Morgann to reveal. But the thought of the two men confronting one another made her stomach churn. She wanted neither of them harmed. For all his flaws, Morgann didn't deserve death and neither did her father. Though he was admittedly just as flawed, if not more. But the years mellowed his warring, greed-driven ways and he was still her father. Blood counted for everything. Her mother had always reminded her of that. Family was the only thing you could rely on in the Highlands.

Sore muscles and stiff thighs soured her mood further as they travelled on. Morgann remained taciturn, barely responding to her gibes. She longed to have some kind of response from him. A shout, an angry grunt, anything! Even a kiss, mayhap. The memory of his scalding kisses made her lips tingle. If only the man would open up to her.

She snorted. He had opened up to her. The memory was still muddled but he'd begged her not to leave him. What had she done to force him to close up again? It twisted at her heart. That man, the one that had sat at her bedside, believing she was dying, was the one she wanted. While her desire wanted the brooding warrior and her mind wanted the friend, her heart longed for the one that so briefly revealed himself to her. That man, she concluded, held her heart. As she lay in bed, listening to his words, she knew she had fallen for him. She loved that man. But if he never came back, then she was loving nothing more than a vague memory.

A strong hand brushed at her cheek, drawing her attention. "The keep is over that hill."

"I remember."

Aye, she remembered the times they used to play there. The Old Castle had been a place to play and, for the men, to train. Their fathers spent much time training their men there, the keep having been abandoned several years past. It was still looked after by the steward of the nearest village for the MacRaes but Alana hadn't returned since the fighting began.

The Old Castle's crenellations peeked over the hill, jagged against the smooth grass of the mountain behind it. Really it was an old manor house. The previous owners built upon it, turning a simple home into one of pretension. The keep had two wings, one jutting forward and one to the side, facing out over the loch. The surrounding walls had long since crumbled and greenery crawled up the side, slowly covering the shutters but the building itself remained strong and sturdy.

Morgann navigated the stone rubble surrounding it easily and brought them up beside the keep. Alana stared up at the building, happy memories mingling with apprehension. She glanced around at the barren scenery. They were truly alone.

And now she was well and truly ruined, she thought with an inward laugh. For what woman would spend time with Morgann MacRae alone and not give herself up to him?

Not that she intended to. Nay, the only man she'd even consider giving herself to was hidden under layers of anger and control.

She twisted around only to find Morgann directly behind her, less than a pace away. As if reading her thoughts, Morgann's intense expression made her throat constrict.

His gaze never left her face as she stumbled back and peered around him at the loch that glimmered in front of the keep. She studied it with more interest than necessary, unwilling to glance at Morgann. She felt his gaze still on her and her pulse fluttered. Stealing a sideways peek at him, a shudder caused her to wrap both arms about her waist. Windswept dark hair, the permanent stubble and that long nose stood out in profile as he too looked over at the loch. Sweet Mary but he was handsome. So rough and wild. She longed to skim her hands over that that bristled jaw, place a finger to his lips and bury her head into his neck to inhale the masculine scent of him. She burned to tame the Highland warrior. If only he would reveal himself to her once more.

"We used to swim in the loch," he said quietly.

"I remember," she replied again.

His head snapped round and that dark gaze fixed on her, narrowing as he studied her expression. Had he heard her wistful tone? Days when life was so much less complicated and a future for them seemed possible certainly held much appeal.

Grabbing the leather bag from his saddle, he tugged on the horse's reins, now tethered to an old wooden beam that once belonged to the stables.

Without another word, he pressed open the heavy door and it groaned in protest as rust fell from the hinges. Motioning for her to enter, he waited for her to climb the steps and flattened a palm to her back, ushering her in. Heat seeped through her gown as the musty smell of stale air greeted her.

The hall hadn't changed. Morgann threw open one of the shutters and proceeded to release the rest. Dust swirled in the air but wood waited in the fire for them and the table was set up in the middle, ready for guests. She strolled about, fingering the carvings of the large chair at the end of the table. The quiet emptiness made her chest feel hollow and then Morgann moved behind her and all at once, her heart felt too full.

"There should be some food supplies in the stores, though I'll have to put the fishing nets out later."

"Aye," she murmured, keeping her gaze on the chair.

Being unaccompanied in Morgann's company was suddenly very intimidating. She felt vulnerable and unsure. It was easy enough to argue and fight against him at Glencolum but now they were alone he could do anything.

And what scared her most was what she wanted him to do to her.

"I'll check if the bed is ready and light the candles."

"Mmm-hmm."

"Do ye need anything?"

"Nay."

"Alana?"

She swallowed and faced him. "Aye?"

"I dinnae know what to do with ye," he admitted. "I dinnae wish to keep ye locked away but ye must see 'tis the only way."

His admission softened her but she didn't want him to see as much so she strode past into the back chamber. It took up the entire left wing of the keep, facing out onto the loch. Though the furnishings were old, the bed looked recently made, ready for their visit. Morgann must have sent on word of their imminent arrival. The blue and red patterned canopy matched the tapestry that covered the rear wall.

Alana sniffed the stale air and opened the shutters in the chamber. The day had turned grim, rain pattering into the mud, creating ripples in the surface of the loch and bringing a fresh scent into the air.

"Where will ye sleep? In the servant's quarters?"

The servant's quarters were accessible only by a door in the side of the keep. Alana shuddered, grateful she wouldn't have to brave the miserable weather to get to her bed.

"Nay, I'll be sleeping here."

Alana set her jaw. "Nay, I'll no' have it. 'Tis bad enough that I shared a chamber with ye at Glencolum but I willnae allow it here, not while we're alone."

He folded his arms across his chest, legs apart, expression determined. "Ye have little choice, lass, unless yer wanting to sleep in the kitchens."

She huffed. "Ye've all but ruined me ye know? No man will ever want me now."

Morgann chuckled as he pressed a hand to the bed, testing the mattress. "Any man that refuses ye must surely be mad."

Warmth seeped up her neck. Had he just complimented her? Oh, aye, he'd kissed her and looked at her with such carnality but never spoken of his attraction to her. Sometimes it seemed so one-sided. Like now, as he strolled around the bed and eyed her. All she could think of was how he'd look sprawled on the bed, hair mussed, the sheets around his hips.

She spun away, a hand to her cheek. Where did these thoughts come from? It was bad enough she was plagued by heated dreams but to be considering such things during the light of day...? He *had* ruined her. Mayhap her reputation would survive but she doubted those thoughts would ever leave.

"Ye need not worry, Alana." He was behind her now. He must have stepped softly as she hadn't heard him approach. "No one will question yer behaviour, only mine."

Chewing her lip, she turned to face him. He stood a mere pace away and his presence sucked the air from her lungs. She would never tire of tracing the line of his shoulders in his linen shirt or studying taut skin just visible at the collar. She sighed. "Ye speak as if ye regret what ye've done."

He curled his fist into a ball but said nothing.

"Yer a good man, Morgann. Send me back and make things right."

"I willnae."

"Morgann—"

"Ye mistake me, Alana. I am no' a good man. I'm a thief."

"Nay—"

He took a step forward and she shrank back as he glowered down at her. "I took that ring."

She swallowed, mouth dry as she struggled to form a response. He took the ring? She shook her head slowly. "Nay..."

Morgann wrenched up his sleeve and thrust his scarred arm in her face. "Look at it, Alana. This is who I am. Look at it and remember. I am naught but a thief. I took that ring just as I took ye. And I'd do it again."

Icy coldness filled her. All this time she'd been convinced her father had been wrong, that Morgann would never steal and now he was saying he had? How foolish she must have sounded. Dropping her gaze, she shoved away from him and strode into the hall.

Alana snatched the bag on the table and began unpacking the few supplies they'd brought. *Bread, ale, dried fruit, a spare gown...* She emptied them all out onto the surface and stared around the uninhabited hall. Swallowing the knot in her throat, she pretended to be absorbed in checking their provisions as Morgann stormed through the room.

"Going to put the fishing nets out," he muttered as he swished past her.

As she took her gown into the bedroom and tucked it into a chest filled with extra bedding, she sighed. He'd lied. And thieved. But why? He had no need of riches and Morgann was never a dishonest man. Aye, she was probably too trusting, too willing to see the good in people when she was younger but she was never a fool and she *knew* Morgann, knew how much pride and honour meant to him. To be branded as a thief would have been the ultimate humiliation so why had he risked it?

She slammed the lid of the chest down. Ach, damn the man! There was so much more to this than he was telling her. If only he would allow himself to open up to her once more. She so longed for those days when they shared everything. Life was simpler then.

Her heart skipped as she glanced over at the bed, its sheets and blankets perfectly made. If only their relationship were simpler too. It would be easier to deal with him if this burning attraction didn't plague her. She probably wouldn't even care what secrets he held from her if she cared little for him. Unfortunately her attraction to him wasn't simple. It seared at her, it tormented her. That little voice of doubt suggested that her childhood friend lay just beneath that beautifully raw exterior and if she let herself, both sides of him could lay claim to her heart for good.

Lip tucked between her teeth, she stared briefly out at the loch, catching sight of Morgann wading out into the water with two small fishing nets, before studying the bed.

And now she'd have to share a bed with him. She shook her head and released a mocking laugh. With the incessant heated dreams she was having, how would she control herself once she lay next to the real thing?

CHAPTER EIGHT

Arms folded, Tèile took up her position on the windowsill and studied the sleeping couple. This was becoming unbearable. She'd not called for help from the Pillywiggins only for them to end up arguing again. And now she was going to be in grave trouble for asking for aid when Alana was poisoned. But what else could she do? Let the lass die?

Thankfully the Pillywiggins were happy to have a green faery in their debt. She *humphed* aloud. The little flower faeries had great control over life and death and thankfully they liked Alana who always enjoyed nature. But who knew what they would ask of her in return for saving her life. Still at least they were on their own now. No more evil witches or attractive cousins getting in their way. Surely now was the time they would finally realise how strong the pull was between them. With each day, their souls grew closer. Each one slowly opened to the other. But there was not much time. She couldn't keep Morgann's messengers in limbo forever and the sleeping spell cast over the Campbells would wear off soon. Already there was too much magic floating around.

She flicked a weary hand toward the two of them. Another dream. Mayhap that would do the trick.

***

Soft, supple flesh gave way as he slipped a hand over her chemise. Alana whimpered in his ear as he teased a nipple, her delicate breast filling his hand perfectly. Hunger shot through him. So perfect, so special. He shifted closer on his side until her thigh pressed into him and switched his attention to her other breast. Morgann's hand shook as he fought to control himself, a savage need rolling through him.

Then he slipped his hands down, tracing the contours of her ribs and stomach through the linen. He inhaled as he met the flesh of her hips, her shift having slipped up to expose her to him. Pressing his hand beneath her, he cupped her bottom, the give of her tender flesh making him groan. She wriggled in invitation and he skimmed his fingers toward the apex of her thighs.

He paused as wet heat greeted him and he blinked.

Damnation, it wasn't a dream. He shot upward. Alana writhed against his hand. Her features were just visible and she clearly slept on, even as his fingers rested over her folds.

"Dinnae stop," she breathed. "Pray dinnae stop."

God's blood, how could he resist? She needed pleasure as much as he needed to give it. He pressed experimentally, blood rushing through his skull as she bucked into his fingers. Morgann moved the pad of one finger carefully, praying for her to sleep on yet yearning for her to awaken. Around and around he circled with the lightest of touches. Sweat tingled on his brow, his body tight as he watched her respond to each movement. Such passion, such beauty. He should have known she'd be like this.

He pushed harder as she writhed. Did she dream of him as he brought her pleasure? Did she imagine him touching her inside and out? Or did she dream of someone else? The thought made his gut clench and made him more determined to help her reach the peak.

Alana curled her hands around the sheets, breasts thrusting upwards. Powerless to stop himself, he leaned over, put his mouth around one firm nipple and sucked at it through the fabric. She pulsed under his fingers and breathed his name, her legs juddering as a sharp release took hold of her.

He grinned. She *had* been dreaming of him. As she sagged back down, Morgann drew away tentatively, hopeful she'd awaken and reward him with a look of satisfaction. A hand lay by her side, slightly open and he tucked his fingers in them briefly as her breathing steadied and she fell into a deeper sleep.

With a sigh, he rolled over and slipped a hand under the pillow. How was he meant to resist the lass now? The scent of her lingered in the air, the sound of her breaths teased him. There was a gap between them yet the heat from her skin traversed it. He only hoped Margot was found soon. This waiting was killing him. He longed to be out there, hunting her down, but who could he trust to protect Alana? No one. But he wasn't so sure he could trust himself now. He just had to control himself for a short while. When this was all over...

He sighed again. When this was all over would he claim her as his or let her go? She'd fought him every step of the way, would she even wish to stay by his side? She'd barely uttered two words to him that eve, not even enough to protest sharing a bed with him. If he'd been inclined to play the chivalrous man, he'd have brought up a pallet from the kitchens and slept on the floor but the castle was cold and he was unable to resist lying next to her. After all, if she didn't forgive him for his treachery, he might never see her again once he returned her to her father.

Morgann battled these thoughts all night, images of Alana naked and sensual in his arms mingling with thoughts of losing her. He woke with a thick head and gritty eyes. Alana, however, awoke with a smile on her face and he fought to keep the knowing grin from his face, in spite of his bad mood.

She quickly covered her smile, affecting a cool look and greeting him with an even cooler, "Good morrow."

Still cross with him then.

"Good morrow, lass. Did ye sleep well?" He rolled out of bed and stretched. Her gaze darted up to his chest briefly, cheeks filling with colour as she tugged the sheets around her.

"Aye, well enough," she replied quietly.

By some miracle, he kept his smug response to himself and dressed quickly. "I've to check the nets. Can ye wait to break yer fast until then?" he asked as he sat to tie his boots.

"Aye, I'll slice some bread while ye do that."

He paused as he glanced up at her. Golden hair tangled around her shoulders, having escaped her braid during the night. She kept the sheets tucked under her chin and her cheeks were rosy. She was so damned exquisite, it near stole his breath.

As he left the bedroom, the peculiar domestic routine they'd found themselves in struck him. And what was stranger, was, in spite of the fact she probably hated him for his lies, he enjoyed it. For the first time in a long time, he only had to worry about himself and Alana.

Stepping out of the hall, he paused at the top of the stairs and drew in a breath. The day was fresh but not too cold. As he gazed out over the loch, the water so still the mountains reflected almost perfectly in it, he realised now was the time. He needed to tell Alana the truth. She was stronger than he ever imagined and in his bid to protect her from the truth, he'd only pushed her away. But no more. He wanted to close the distance between them for once and for all. If she couldn't forgive him or didn't believe him, then so be it, but at least he'd know.

With easy strides, he came to the water's edge and dipped to scoop some up, the freezing water clearing away his fatigue as he scrubbed his face and hair. Morgann ran his fingers through his hair and removed his boots before wading up to the nets. He lifted them. Not bad. They wouldn't starve at least.

He went to pull the net to the bank and halted as a splash of cold water hit his back, trickling through his shirt. He turned to see Alana, skirts in hand, ankle deep in the water, an impish smile on her face.

One brow raised, he eyed her and dropped the net. "What are ye playing at, lass?"

"Naught." She lifted her chin and swished her gown playfully.

He frowned. "Yer not angry with me anymore?"

"I was never angry, Morgann. Just annoyed. Ye made a fool of me, ye know? I protested yer innocence for so long."

"So 'tis not the fact that I'm a thief that bothers ye, just yer hurt pride?"

Alana tilted her head. "Ye may think of me as a daft lass, laird, but I am no fool. Whatever ye did, ye had good reason to. Yer no' a heartless thief, any more than I'm a naïve lass."

Taking a moment to study her, he shook his head. When was it she became so wise? And how did she see through him so easily?

"Will ye not tell me, Morgann? Tell me why ye took the ring, why ye took me."

He grimaced. As much as he'd been prepared to tell all, he didn't relish sharing her father's sordid deeds with her. "Aye, but get out of the water first. I'll no' have ye catching a chill."

With a roll of her eyes, she stepped out onto the shingled bank and he followed her, fighting the urge to scoop her up and protect her bare feet from the stones. She folded her arms across her chest and glared at him as he rolled down his sleeves. "Well?"

Her gaze connected with his, green eyes imploring him for the truth. Lord knows he wanted to unburden himself. And Alana was so much stronger than he ever realised.

"That ring..." He coughed. "That ring was my mothers. A ring of promise given to her by my father."

She blinked. "So why did my father have it?"

"My stepmother gave it to yer father as a promise too. A promise that she would become his bride as soon as my father was dead."

Alana's mouth parted but she remained silent.

"She intended for my father to die very soon after she made that promise. I found out about her plans by accident one night and I think I prevented her from killing him as she'd hoped. By poison."

"So that's why ye think I was…"

"Aye. Poison seems to be Margot's weapon of choice." He fisted his hands by his side, jaw tight as he considered how close he'd been to losing Alana. "I heard Margot speaking with her lady-in-waiting one night. Once my father was dead, she planned to rise up with yer father and take the MacRae lands. With my father dead and her holding the land she'd inherit as his wife, 'twould have been an easy victory. I wasnae fit for leading a war at that age to be sure."

"Sweet Mary," she whispered. "But the ring… why take it?"

"My father wanted proof. Margot insisted the ring had been stolen. She even had a servant girl punished for it. I thought if I could bring it back, he would see she was lying and she'd be forced to confess all. I'll admit my plans were no' the best but I did what I thought I had to."

"Oh, Morgann, ye should have said something. I could have got that ring for ye easily.

He gave her a tilted grin. "I didnae want ye knowing what yer father was up to. I thought ye'd be heartbroken." He studied her as she took it in, shoulders straight, chin raised. As strong as ever. "I was wrong, was I not?"

She let slip a small smile. "I dinnae know. I'm no' daft, I was always aware of my father's ways. He always wanted more. More land, more power. It never occurred to me he might have his eye on yer lands though. But he isnae the same now, Morgann. Even if Margot succeeded in her plans, he's too old to be fighting wars."

"She still wants my father dead. And ye. Yer the key here, Alana. With ye, I intended to force yer father to admit the truth and to ensure Margot's true nature was revealed."

Alana pressed her lips together and shook her head. "Ye know, if ye'd just asked…"

He let out a snort. "Aye… would ye believe that I thought I was protecting ye?"

Head tilted, she scrutinised him and his pulse thumped under her penetrating gaze. She didn't seem angry. Or disappointed. Or anything he'd expected. Ach, he could hardly believe he'd spent all this time fearing telling her and here she was, taking the news with such calm control. He'd underestimated the lass severely.

But no longer. Nay, he knew what Alana was made of and, by God, did it serve to increase his desire for her. For a woman like Alana would surely be able to match any man, especially a Highlander. He loved her, he realised. Mayhap he always had.

"Morgann MacRae," she declared suddenly. "Yer as stubborn

a man as I've ever met. But, aye, I believe ye thought it best. But now we have the truth, I can help ye. Return me home and I'll speak with my da. I'll persuade him to tell all to yer father."

He took in her stubborn chin, the determined glint in her eyes. "Aye. Aye, I believe ye will."

Hell fire, the lass could persuade a whole army to give up their fight and return home, he suspected. Who in their right mind could resist a creamy skinned, flaxen-haired goddess with more fortitude than a dozen men?

"So ye'll return me home?"

"Soon enough," he replied cryptically. He wasn't sure he could bear to part with her too soon and Margot was still on the loose. How could he protect her if she returned home?

"Ach, what am I to do with ye, MacRae?"

He grinned and let his gaze rove lazily over her. "I could think of a few things, *Campbell*."

Cheeks brightening as she gave a startled gasp, she jumped forward and shoved him back. Taken by surprise, he stumbled back, landing hard on the bank, half submerged in the water.

"Mayhap that will cool ye off," she declared.

Morgann swiped the water from his face and tried to affect a glower but he must have failed as Alana didn't look at all intimidated. Nay, she looked vibrant and happy and disturbingly like everything he'd ever wanted. He rose up onto his elbows as she eyed him, daring him to retaliate. He leaped up and gave chase, determined she'd get a good soaking too. Her laughter rang out as she sprinted away, lifting his heart.

Ach, he doubted all the lochs in Scotland could cool his need for her.

***

The shutters crashed against the castle as she threw them open. A clear sky greeted her and the gentle breeze cooled her skin. But it could not cool her thoughts. These dreams were coming every night now and were becoming more and more heated. She glanced at the bed, eyeing the rumpled sheets and the indent where Morgann had lain.

Where was he? In spite of the heat the dream had caused it was still a cold night so she didn't know why he'd left her bed. The tangled bedding sparked a memory of hard masculine flesh crawling across them. It wasn't real but, sweet Mary, her dream had been vivid. The way his body aligned with hers. The way he took her mouth so fiercely. Her stomach fluttered at the thought.

She couldn't sleep. Not after everything Morgann had told her. It made sense. Her father had been power-hungry in his younger years and Margot was certainly an experienced seductress. Not many men would refuse her.

Except Morgann. After their day together, catching fish and cooking them by the loch, a fresh sense of hope pervaded her.

That was the man she loved.

Foolish, stubborn man that he was. So many years wasted. If he'd only told her of his worries, she was sure she could right them. But a highlander didn't rely on a mere lass. Nay, they were taught to protect the weak and deal with their problems on their own. In spite of his idiocy, she couldn't help but admire him all the more for bearing his troubles alone.

She leaned further out the window, seeking the relief of the fresh night air. Stars dotted the skies, reflected in the loch. The flat inky black surface mirrored the sky so well that Alana was half tempted to run down and jump in and pretend she was bathing with the stars.

A movement in the water caught her attention, a ripple that caused the pinpricks of light to bob and weave. Alana squinted at the spot. A gasp wedged in her throat as a person surfaced. Nay, not a person. *Morgann.* His shoulders breached the water, the shadowy surface shrinking away to reveal his chest as if birthing him from the gloom. If she didn't know better she'd think him some dark and sinister being.

But no monster could look like that. Indeed he still looked dangerous but the danger was more likely to her heart than her body.

Nay, mayhap the danger was to both.

Her mouth grew dry and she realised she watched with an open mouth. Nails digging into the stone windowsill, she found herself unable to turn away as he continued to stalk toward the edge of the loch.

Lean hips came next and her cheeks flamed as she eyed the shadows at the juncture of his thighs. Alana scolded herself for wishing the light was better. Muscles flexed and rippled as he stepped completely from the water and reached for something. His plaid by the looks of it.

Disappointment struck her as he wrapped it about his hips and grasped it in one hand. Still, she took a moment to study his torso. Her dreams, as heated as they had been, had done him little justice. As he moved closer to the keep, she made out the dark hair that swirled over his chest, leading down his firm stomach in invitation.

Before she had a chance to think on it, Alana spun away and flung open the door to the chambers. She scurried along the hall to the front entrance and paused, heart thumping as she waited. What *was* she doing?

Legs frozen, she listened as wet feet slapped against the stone steps. What would she even say to him? Her chest grew tight as the door creaked open slowly. He was likely trying to be quiet so as not to wake her. She dropped her gaze to the floor, unsure what on Earth she was going to say to him.

Water pattered gently onto the wooden floorboards as he stepped in. Before she could utter a word, he was upon her, one strong hand wrapped around her throat and he thrust her back against the wall. She tried to scream but his grip was too powerful and it came out as a muffled sound. He bore down on her and plunged a hand into her hair, yanked her head up.

The rage in his expression made her insides shrivel in fear and she went limp against his hold, the pressure from his hand making her neck ache. Morgann dropped both hands suddenly and she sagged against the wall.

"Alana? Hell fire!"

Alana blinked, a hand to her neck as she swallowed her fear.

"Did I hurt ye? Forgive me, 'twas dark. I didn't think. I thought ye were Margot. God's teeth, forgive me."

He reached out and she shrank back. But it wasn't fear she felt anymore. As he'd grabbed her, he'd dropped his plaid and he now stood completely naked. While she remained in the shadows, the starlight streaming through the door highlighted him perfectly. She saw everything. From his large masculine feet, to his muscular thighs, to his manhood.

She tilted her head slightly. His manhood that appeared to be growing. Heat flourished in her chest and she put a hand to it. Oh dear Lord. And she couldn't seem to drag her gaze away.

"Alana, are ye well? Did I hurt ye? Talk to me, lass."

Snapping her eyes up, she shook her head frantically, unable to find enough her voice to even utter a simple 'nay'.

"What were ye doing, lass?"

Of its own accord, her gaze slipped down to the apex of his

thighs and she gulped, the sound seeming loud in her ears. Mayhap he'd heard it too as he cursed and darted a look around. He spied his plaid, snatched it up and flung it lazily around his hips, fisting it in one hand.

"I-I couldnae sleep," she squeaked, suddenly finding what was left of her voice. "What were ye doing?" she added accusingly.

Aye, why was he swimming in the middle of the night and teasing her with his warrior's body?

"Cooling off," he replied easily, inching closer. Morgann reached out and brushed a thumb across her throat, soothing the spot where his fingers had pressed.

She scowled. "'Tis nae hot."

He grinned suddenly, teeth flashing in the dark and mischievous Morgann made himself known. "'Tis when I share a bed with ye."

"Oh."

They both fell silent as his thumb continued to play across her throat. The coarse fingertip against her skin made her shiver as she stared up at him. Hair hung over his face, still wet and spiked and dark eyes peeked out from underneath it, his lashes wet too. It made her want to reach out and brush his hair away, to smooth a palm across his cheek and savour the rough texture but she remained rigid, fearful of making the wrong move and ending the moment. It seemed fate had been leading up to this point and everything was suddenly very clear.

All this time life forced her into Morgann's arms. As if they were being given a second chance. They'd missed out on their time together all those years ago and now this was it. They'd both changed but this day had proved to her there was more to Morgann than surly moods and a gruff manner. Buried deep inside was her friend. She'd seen him briefly when they'd played around in the loch.

And on the outside was a beautiful, fierce man. Both combined made her weak at the knees.

A drop of water splashed on her cheek as it dripped from his hair and it made her jolt as she realised just how close he was. Somehow he now stood so near that she could feel the heat radiating from his chest. She had to crane her neck to look up at him.

"Did I hurt ye?" he asked again, his voice gruff.

"Nay." Her voice sounded just as gruff to her ears.

"I couldnae forgive myself if I did. I've never wanted to hurt ye, Alana. Everything I've done has been to protect ye, ye know."

She nodded dumbly as he closed the gap with agonising slowness. She gasped as his body squashed her breasts, her nipples instantly pebbling. He kept coming, pressing into her until not a whisper of air could fit between them. His hard thighs rasped against her chemise.

She whimpered. His hand left her throat. His mouth took its place.

Warmth and delicious sensations curled through her as Morgann opened his lips against her neck and flicked his tongue across her skin. She leaned away, giving him better access and he trailed kisses up and down the side of her neck.

She wrapped both arms around his neck and toyed with the damp hair there. One of his hands plunged under her hair, tugged it high, completely exposing her shoulder to him. Morgann jerked lightly on her chemise with the other hand and it slipped down, hanging just above her breasts.

And then that hand was upon one of her breasts, comforting and teasing at the same time. He cupped her through the linen, rolled her nipple tight. He groaned against the crook of her shoulder and teeth nipped lightly at her skin.

"Ye taste so good," he murmured. "So good."

Alana arched to his touch and angled her hips into him. Hardness greeted her, his plaid gone, as an ache took hold, one that could only be ended by Morgann. The scent of damp skin teased as his wet hair brushed her cheek. He pulled away suddenly, hand still clasped over her breast, fingers remaining under her hair.

"I cannae do it." His eyes were hooded, dark with lust, voice thick and emotion filled.

Alana's heart dropped. She leaned her head back, let the air release from her chest and dropped her hands to her side.

"I cannae do it, Alana. I cannae stay away from ye. I wanted to protect ye, to be strong for ye... I dinnae think I can be strong anymore."

Relief streamed through her. He wasn't turning her down. She placed her palm over his heart, the thud strong, reassuring. "Dinnae be strong, Morgann. Just be ye. And kiss me."

He gave a groan of resignation and the hand on her breast advanced around behind her, bundled her against him. Lips moved roughly over hers, claiming, seeking. He coaxed her mouth apart and the damp heat of his tongue shocked her, forced her to grip his arms tightly. Sinuously twining with her tongue, he explored every recess of her mouth as fire built between them. The throb between her thighs became more acute, almost painful. She rocked her hips into him to get some kind of relief.

Morgann pulled her away from the wall and his hands roamed her body. The linen chemise offered little protection against his probing hands as he grasped her bottom, fingers trailing briefly between her thighs and back up. Alana kept her eyes closed as he manoeuvred her around the room, mouth firmly upon hers, until finally the edge of the table bit into the back of her thighs.

Hands gliding over the planes of his chest, she opened her

eyes and reclined. She'd intended to study him, to relish the sight of firm muscles and crisp hair but to see him, so gut-wrenchingly beautiful, a vulnerable glint in his eyes, forced a surge of impatient need through her.

"Kiss me again," she begged, hooking a hand around his neck and tugging him down.

He did as she bid. His mouth moved sensuously over hers yet there was an aggression behind the kiss. A sense of him taking everything from her. But he gave back so much. His fingers pressed into her hip, massaging her flesh. She fidgeted, longing for those fingers to put an end to her agony.

"Morgann..." she keened, unsure of what she begged for now. Only he could know.

He ripped his mouth from hers, pushing both hands across her cheeks and holding her face. Their breaths echoed through the vast room. "I need ye, *mo ghràidh.* I need ye more than my next breath."

"Aye." She nodded frantically, hooking her legs around his thighs in an attempt to close the distance again. "Aye," was all she could say again.

"I'll no' take ye here."

Firm hands pressed under her bottom and Morgann lifted her easily into his hold. He coaxed her legs around him, his sex pressed firmly against her tender flesh. So much restrained power made her shudder and she hid her face in his neck as he carried her effortlessly into the rear chamber.

Blankets enveloped her as he laid her down with a tenderness that stretched her heart. Candlelight gilded his skin, sharpening the shadows in his features, and highlighting each indent of muscle. She reached out and traced a finger over his stomach, drawing a hiss from him.

"Did ye light the candles?" she whispered, grateful to be able to see him properly but wondering how he had time to light them as he carried her in.

His brow creased. "Nay, I thought ye did."

"Nay," she replied softly, her confusion dissipating as he stroked a finger down her cheek, all thoughts forgotten at his tender touch. She continued to explore his body with her hand as he propped himself over her, weight held on one arm.

Morgann snatched her hand and laid it carefully back on the bed. "Dinnae touch me, lass." He grinned at her disappointed expression. "Just for a little while. I need to see ye, need to touch ye. Slowly, gently. I dinnae think I can if ye touch me. 'Twill be over too soon."

She licked her lips, swallowing at the promise in his gaze as his hand reached down to the hem of her chemise, currently tangled around her thighs. He glanced down as he inched the fabric higher. Her breaths grew erratic as anticipation built. Morgann shifted to press it up to her waist, hunger clear in his eyes.

And then he swept the chemise clean over her head and parts of his body moulded to hers. Not enough of him touched her really and she longed to draw him down and feel his full weight but she somehow managed to keep her hands to herself, curling them into the sheets.

Morgann's gaze roved over her. Every part of her scalded. Her stomach knotted and her skin grew sensitised. She pressed her thighs together. A hand reached down to draw up her ankle, making her bend her leg. Rough fingers explored the arch of her foot, then the back of her knee and the responsive skin on her inner thigh. She quivered and quaked with each touch, small sounds that she had no control over escaping her.

"Alana." His voice cracked at the end of her name. "Sweet Lord, I had no idea... yer too good for me. A more beautiful lassie I've never seen."

Alana beamed at his words, tears of delight tingling in her eyes. She meant to respond but his fingers continued their journey over her body and she forgot how to speak. Squeezing briefly at her hips, he teased a finger over her stomach, dipped into her belly button before he skimmed her ribs and settled over one breast.

Her back left the bed at the exquisite feel of rugged male flesh on her own soft skin. She gazed at him as he teased her nipple. Lowering his head, he took it into his mouth.

"Oh!"

By God, if he made her feel like that with just his mouth… Sharp heat around her breast made her head swim as he flicked her nipple with his tongue and sucked leisurely at it. He nipped briefly with his teeth, a sweet contrast to his soothing licks.

"*Mo chridhe*," he murmured as his lips tickled over her skin, tracing her collarbone before seeking her mouth.

The endearment destroyed any remaining restraint and her hands flew around his shoulders, pinning him. A faint growl emanated from Morgann as he took her mouth. He pressed a hand under her back, moulding her to him as he kissed her with such intensity that her head spun. Gone was his teasing touch and careful restraint. The warrior remained, the one that her body sought with a need so ancient it made her shake.

She tried to match his kisses as their teeth clashed and they fought to get closer. Her legs fell apart and he pumped his hips against her, mimicking the act she craved most. She scrabbled her nails across his smooth back, feeling each ripple of movement as he winnowed his fingers through her hair. Her skin grew hot and damp as they rocked furiously, frissons of pleasure sparking between her legs. She arched and arched into him, steely flesh pressing across her folds until all breath left her and she let out a cry, one that Morgann muffled with a penetrating kiss. Gratification spiralled out through her limbs and she quaked as the feelings simmered into a warm satisfaction.

Sweet Mary, who knew? But then she must have done or else she would not have craved his touch so much.

Morgann kept on kissing her, hot open-mouthed kisses to her chin, jaw, neck and lips as the need for him grew again. Instead of dissipating, the longing increased, powered by the knowledge of what pleasure he could bring. She needed to join with him.

"Now," she whispered. "Morgann. Now." She pressed her juncture into him.

"Aye, *m'eudail*, aye." He wrapped her legs around his hips and grasped her bottom in one hand, the other stoking her cheek as he supported his weight on his elbow. "I'm going to take ye now, Alana. Make ye mine. I'll try to be gentle, but I dinnae... I dinnae know if I can," he told her roughly.

Alana shook her head gently, eyes locked onto his. "Do what ye will with me, Morgann. Make me yers. I'm no' scared."

She wasn't. Nothing could prevent her from wanting this. If her voice shook and her heart hammered, it was only with desperation. As he had claimed of her, she needed him more than her next breath.

He inched forward, hot flesh spreading her apart and her eyes widened as he took her. Carefully, slowly, tenderly. And then he was buried to the hilt and Alana gasped at the unknown sensation budding inside her. He waited. And she fidgeted, the need to move overriding any discomfort.

"God's blood, Alana," he said through gritted teeth, "so tight."

She wriggled again and watched as any final restraint slipped away. A dark, feral light grew in his eyes as he shifted against her. She felt the hammer of his heart against her chest as he withdrew and plunged deeply, as if testing her. Alana released a moan of appreciation and the sound seemed to trigger something.

Fingers digging into her bottom, Morgann drove into her with deep, hard strokes. Alana could do nothing but hold on as he made her his. Each thrust had her calling his name, begging for an end yet wanting it to last forever. As the rapture built, Morgann drew back, dark gaze latched onto hers. His image grew hazy but Alana saw the desire—and the love?—in his expression and she dug her nails into his skin as she bucked upwards.

With a hoarse groan, he plunged several more times, carrying her over the edge. Her body pulsed and quivered and he followed her over, kissing her shakily as he released inside her. She soothed him through it, rubbing her hands over his sleek skin and spreading kisses over his jawline, tasting the saltiness of his skin.

He flopped down beside her, still joined, a hand coming up to clasp possessively over her breast. Morgann nuzzled into her neck and nipped at her ear. "Ah, *mo chridhe*, what shall I do with ye?" he asked softly.

Alana grinned, still massaging lazily at his back. "I could think of a few things."

He came up onto his elbow and his boyish expression grew serious. "I didnae hurt ye, did I?"

"Nay." She reached up and swept his hair from his face. "'Twas wonderful."

His gave her a tilted smile. "I should have been more careful but ye do something to me, Alana. I cannae control myself around ye."

"Ye dinnae need to control yerself around me, Morgann. Ye can let go sometimes, ye know?"

With a shake of his head, he eased himself away from her and settled her into the crook of his thighs, an arm wrapped around her waist. Strong legs brushed hers as he cocooned her with his body. Alana allowed herself a satisfied smile. She didn't know what the future held for them but everything had changed now. For the better.

"How come ye understand me so well, lass?"

She shrugged. "Yer my best friend. Eight summers cannae change that."

"I'm yer lover too now."

"Aye, that ye are."

He swept aside her hair and brushed a kiss across the back

of her neck, sending a shiver down her spine. "Will ye let me love ye some more?"

"Aye." She let slip a moan as a hand slid between her legs. "Aye, love me some more, Morgann MacRae."

CHAPTER NINE

Wincing as the floorboards creaked, Morgann stepped carefully across the floor to throw open the shutters. Daylight streamed in. The day proved to be clear but cold, a thick blanket of clouds covering the sky. But the day could not seem more beautiful to Morgann. Ach, he still had the grin of a fool on his face.

He glanced at Alana and tiptoed to the bed. One sweet breast peeked out of the sheets and he settled beside her. Even as the bed dipped under his weight, she slept on. Male pride filled him. He'd well and truly worn her out, insatiable woman that she was.

Hooking a finger under the sheet, he slid it down, waiting for her to awaken. When she showed no signs of stirring, he grew bolder and slipped the sheets from her body. He admired her creamy skin, slender thighs, the indent of her waist. Red marks graced her where his stubble had scratched her. He regretted marring her delicate skin but a part of him liked the thought of marking her as his. He ached to touch but feared waking her. She looked so perfect, so peaceful, he couldn't bring himself to disturb that. Was there any better look than that of a satisfied woman?

Ach, but he'd met his match in Alana. Mayhap he shouldn't have given in but he didn't regret it. Somehow he would make everything right. Somehow he would persuade Laird Dougall to let him marry Alana. He'd taken her now. Dougall could hardly deny him his right to her.

And nothing on Earth could make him let her go now. He only hoped giving into his desire hadn't put her in danger. He still needed to remain focused until Margot had been caught and there had still been no word from Finn. Or Alana's father. It was as if the man didn't even care his daughter was missing.

Unable to resist any longer, he touched one rosy nipple, his scowl quickly turning into a smile as she released a small moan. Did she dream of him? Lord knows, he dreamed of her often enough. But the reality proved far better than he ever imagined.

Her eyelids fluttered open, an inviting smile on her face. "Good morrow," she said softly, voice still husky from sleep.

"Good morrow."

Need, deep and powerful rolled through him as she

stretched with no concern for her naked state. Her eyes widened as her gaze fixed onto his face. She parted her legs in silent invitation. Blood roared in his ears as she offered herself up to him.

Thoughts of slow and careful vanished and he settled swiftly between her thighs, pushing them further apart. He resisted the urge to kiss her, wanting to see her face in the daylight as he took her. He filled her in one movement, delighting in her strangled gasp and large green eyes.

Driven by pure primitive instinct, he left her no time to adjust as he merged with her. Alana gripped at his rear, urging him closer as her fiery heat consumed him.

"Aye, take me, Morgann. Make me yers."

He shuddered as her words echoed his thoughts and he moved relentlessly inside her. He wouldn't last long but neither would she. Already she quivered around him, on the cusp of a climax. Something elemental held them both captive and her eyes clouded with tears.

"Dinnae cry," he soothed, even as he kept up his brutal pace. "I love ye, Alana."

"I. Love. Ye. Too," she ground out as her passion crested.

Her words and her spasms took him by surprise, a searing explosion that had him rasping her name. The gratification ebbed, leaving behind a warm satisfaction and a grin on his face.

Alana's lips quirked as he stared down at her, aware he probably looked a fool.

"Yer a scoundrel, Morgann MacRae."

"Aye, but I'm yer scoundrel."

She traced a finger across his jawline. "Aye, I suppose ye are."

"Ye suppose?" He pressed up onto his hands and tried to look offended. "Ye dinnae need to make it sound like a hardship. There's no 'suppose' about it. Yer mine now, Alana. Just as I'm yers."

"As ye will." She released a light laugh.

"I'll be marry—" He paused and turned as someone pounded at the door. "Ach, who could that be?" He clambered off Alana with a scowl as he searched for his shirt. He tugged it on, eyeing Alana as she slipped from the bed, a sheet wrapped around her and held in one hand. "Dinnae go anywhere," he ordered. "Stay here and shut the door."

"But—"

"Dinnae argue with me, lass. Stay here and stay naked."

She slapped playfully at his arm as he fastened his plaid and slipped into his boots. As she slumped onto the bed, sheet still wrapped loosely around her, he shook his head. A more tempting sight he'd never seen. Tousled hair, bare shoulders, slender legs peeking out from the cotton sheet. Hell, he wanted her again. He only hoped this was Finn with some good news. If they'd finally caught Margot he could hand her to Dougall for punishment and request Alana's hand. There was no way the man would forgive Margot for nearly killing his only daughter and any talk of an alliance between Margot and Dougall would be finished. The MacRae lands would be out of danger and Morgann would have Alana as his own.

Hopefully.

The hammering continued as he carefully closed the chamber door behind him, stealing one last peek at Alana as she pouted in mock annoyance.

"Aye, aye, I'm coming." He stomped across the hall floor and threw open the door. A young brown-haired lad, no more than eighteen summers stood in the doorway.

"My laird?"

"Aye, what is it ye want?" Morgann didn't manage to keep the annoyance from his voice. Damnation. He'd really hoped it was Finn. All this waiting was going to drive him mad.

The lad shrank back. "Forgive me, my laird. I've been sent to tell ye that the witch has been spotted."

Hope pressed a smile across his face. "Where, lad?"

"To the east. Past the red hill. There's an old cottage."

Morgann nodded. He knew of the ancient dwelling. He'd ridden past it several times. "I thank ye, lad. What's yer name? I've no' seen ye before."

"I'm from the village. I'm Big Tom."

Turning, Morgann snatched his sword and leather pouch. He fished out a coin and pressed it into Tom's palm. "My thanks. Be off with ye now."

Tom nodded and hurried away. Morgann grinned. Finally he'd bring his stepmother to justice. Finn must have spread the word that he was looking for Margot. He glanced over his shoulder to see Alana stood in the chamber doorway, still wrapped in a sheet.

"Ach, I told ye—"

"Yer going after her then." She bit her lip.

"Aye."

"Be careful, Morgann. I dinnae trust her."

"Nor do I. Which is why I've got to make sure she's caught."

"I fear for ye."

Heart warmed by her concern, Morgann closed the gap between them and rubbed his hands up and down her bare arms. "There's no need for ye to worry, lass. She's no match for me. I'll be back in yer bed before long."

"Ye promise?"

"Aye, I promise. And soon enough I'll have ye for my wife too."

Her beautiful eyes lit with delight. "In truth?"

"Aye, of course. Ye didnae think I'd be letting ye escape me this time, did ye?"

She came up onto her tiptoes and brushed a kiss across his

lip. "Just be sure to come back to me, Morgann."

"I will. I swear it. I'll no' be parted from ye again."

Sweeping her into his arms, he kissed her passionately, sending wave of longing through him again. Would he ever get enough of her? As he pulled away and observed the glazed look of lust in her eyes he decided he probably wouldn't. He released her, ran both hands through his hair and slid his sword through his belt.

"Stay here until I come for ye. No getting into trouble, ye hear?"

Alana nodded as she wrapped her arms around her waist. So vulnerable, so beautiful. He could hardly wait to be back and holding her in his arms once more.

"I love ye," she murmured.

"I love ye too."

He strode outside and mounted his steed, the thrill of the hunt beginning to course through him. With one last nod to Alana, he set his gaze on the horizon and dug his heels into the mount's side. He grinned. Today was proving to be a fine day indeed.

***

Alana pressed a finger to her lips and released a small smile. A faint niggle of concern played at the back of her mind but the gentle ache of her body quickly dampened it. She gave a giggle and strolled back into the chamber, dropped the sheets and studied the marks Morgann had left on her.

Marking her as his.

Ach, what a lovesick fool she was. But she couldn't regret a thing. She just had to persuade her father to say 'aye' to their marriage. He wouldn't deny her surely? For all his faults, he still loved her and always wanted the best for her. And he wasn't that angry, power hungry man anymore. He'd just be happy for her to be looked after.

She hoped.

She slipped into her chemise and tied the ribbon at the neck while remembering how Morgann had pushed it off her. The scent of him still lingered on her skin. She should wash but she liked the thought of smelling of him.

As she picked up her comb, a knock sounded. Lip tucked between her teeth, she placed the comb down. Should she answer it? What if it was something to do with Margot? A warning perhaps. Unease twisted her stomach. If trouble was brewing then she'd have to go after Morgann and warn him.

Snatching her plaid, she threw it over her shoulders and stalked to the door. As she inched it open, something pushed it swiftly back, the heavy wood knocking her to the floor. Dazed, Alana tried to push herself up but a small, leather shoe pressed onto her chest.

"Oh dear," a familiar voice said as Alana followed the leg up.

Light streamed in around the intruder blocking out her features but she knew who it was. She felt the blood leave her face, palms growing sticky. Before she could put up a fight, something swung down at her. Alana raised an arm but was too late. Pain registered, sharp and agonising. She sank gratefully into the darkness crowding her mind.

***

She woke still on the floor, prickly rushes digging into her cheek, her tongue dry and head pounding. Ach, she'd be lucky to have any sense left the amount of times she'd hit her head recently. Except *she* hadn't hit her head. Margot had. Alana threw a look around the hall and spied her in one corner, brushing the rushes into a pile by the door. Alana frowned and winced as she fought to move. Her hands were bound behind her back, ropes chafing her skin, her feet tied together. She pushed out the fabric tied tightly around her mouth with her tongue, finally loosening it enough so that it slipped down her chin.

Margot lifted her head at the sound of rustling and stepped over, tilting her head to study Alana. "Yer awake then." She grinned. "Honestly, I cannae believe Morgann fell for that. I thought him a smart man, but obviously not."

"What do ye want, Margot?" Alana swallowed, tried to erase the dryness in her throat.

"Well, is that no' obvious? I want ye dead. Ye and Morgann."

The delight in the woman's voice, the look in her cold grey eyes made Alana shudder. This was what Morgann had always seen and what Alana always sensed. To see the evil in Margot so close to the surface was truly terrifying.

Alana twisted her wrists in the hopes of loosening the knots. "Why? Why are ye doing this? Just let me go and we'll forget this happened. I'll persuade Morgann to forgive ye."

Margot crouched, letting loose a light laugh. "Morgann will never forgive me. He knows I tried to poison ye. He's always known about me. How ye survived, I dinnae know, but I dinnae intend to let it happen again."

Licking her lips, Alana wriggled again, mind racing. She couldn't be sure why she was still alive but the malicious glint in Margot's eyes told her enough. She *had* to get free. Had to find Morgann and warn him.

She stiffened as Margot trailed a fingernail over her cheek, a twisted smile on her lips. "I still cannae figure out why he fell for ye and not me. Yer pretty enough but... well, Morgann's the first man I've no' been able to seduce. Even yer father was easy. But 'tis no matter. Morgann will regret not falling into bed with me soon enough."

Teeth gritted, Alana sucked in air through her nostrils. "He'll regret naught, only that he didnae catch ye sooner. Ye'll not harm Morgann."

Margot's smile expanded. "We'll see."

The promise behind the words made sent an icy chill through Alana's veins. Whatever Margot had planned, she suspected she'd be used as some kind of trap. It was the only reason for her to be still alive. Mayhap Margot noted the ashen colour of her skin as the woman's smile took on a malicious hint. "Poor Alana. None of this is yer fault, angel. Ye just happened to get caught up in a fight for power and I cannae have ye in the way. I've devoted too much time to this, waited too long."

Margot pushed to standing and lifted a pot from the table. She carried it over to the pile of rushes and poured the contents over them. Alana sniffed. Oil. Bile scorched her throat. Margot planned to burn the keep. With her in it probably. She fought to sit up, her arms aching as she forced herself upright.

"Pray, Margot, dinnae do this." Alana tried to keep her voice strong, only the faintest hint of her fear invading it.

"I do, Alana. Morgann and ye are the only ones standing between me and everything I've ever wanted. Once I marry yer father, I'll bring my land to the marriage contract and the rest of the MacRaes will have to bow to our power."

"My da will never marry ye after this!"

"Aye, he will. Just as we planned. Yer death will be some tragic accident." Margot released a dramatic sigh. "And Morgann's father will never recover from his son's death. I fear the heartbreak will mean the end for him."

"Ye'll not succeed." Alana strained against her bonds. She couldn't let Morgann walk into this, she just couldn't. "Morgann will defeat ye easily. Yer greed as got the better of ye. Just leave while ye can."

Pray, pray leave. The thought of burning to death was bad enough but knowing Morgann was going to walk into a trap near killed her. Her heart hurt. But Morgann was strong and clever. She just prayed Margot would not succeed with whatever she had planned for him.

"Ye dinnae understand, do ye? 'Tis well enough for ye, the pampered daughter of a laird. Ye've got everything. Power, family, love. I have naught."

"Ye have family. The MacRaes took ye in. Ye have love!"

"Ach, from an aged man who loves me for naught more than my body and looks."

"My father willnae love ye. He would never love another after my mother."

Margot sniffed as she stepped closer, the oil carrier swinging from one hand. "I care not now." She stopped in front of Alana and tilted the pot. Alana squealed and scrabbled away as sticky oil trickled over her chemise. Margot laughed. "Funny, Morgann wanted to burn me as a witch but now I'll be burning the both of ye. Fitting, dinnae ye think? My mother was accused of being a witch ye know? Forced out of society. We lived on naught. My mother died a lonely, horrible death. So ye see, Alana, ye'll never understand."

With a gulp, Alana studied the woman as wild delight grew visible in her eyes. "I-I am sorry for what happened to ye," she whispered. "But none of this will bring back yer mother."

Margot laughed. "Nay, nay it won't. But I'll still enjoy it nonetheless."

The woman's excitement sent a rush of anger through her. She'd already tried to kill her once and now she wanted to kill Morgann too. She wouldn't let herself be used to trap him. Jaw set, Alana shook her head. "Yer a coward, Margot. Poison, fires. Ye cannae even bring yerself to kill me." Eyes narrow, Margot backhanded her, hitting her to the floor. Her cheek burned but Alana couldn't prevent the smug smile that crept across her face. "Coward," she repeated quietly.

Spinning, Margot snatched an eating knife from the table and held it out. The tip wavered as it danced in front of Alana. Unable to keep her gaze from the blade, Alana gulped. *Mayhap that wasn't such a good idea.*

CHAPTER TEN

That familiar chill raced up Morgann's spine as something clenched at his heart. That sensation that seemed to link him to Alana. The one that told him she was in trouble. He squeezed the reins. He saw the abandoned cottage ahead, the roof now a skeleton of wooden beams, its walls crumbling. Sat in the middle of the valley on the crest of a hill, it was exposed to the elements. The tugging on his heart grew urgent, almost painful, making his stomach churn. Should he continue on or turn back?

He couldn't see how Alana would be in trouble unless she'd done something foolish again. Mayhap she had made another rash attempt at an escape. He shook his head. Nay, a more content lass he'd never seen. There was no way she'd leave him now. Not after she'd declared her love for him.

The warm sensation as he recalled her sweet words failed to remove the unease from his body and he urged Caraid on. He just had to check the cottage. Just had to be sure Margot wasn't hiding there. It was said the hut once belonged to a witch. He snorted. What could be more fitting? Anyway, how much trouble could Alana really get into in the Old Castle?

Morgann pulled the horse to a stop and leaped from the saddle. The wooden door of the cottage still stood and he shoved it open, leaving it swinging awkwardly on one hinge.

Damnation. Empty.

Either Margot had already left or he'd been sent on a fool's errand.

"Hell's teeth!"

Racing back to his mare, he mounted and forced her into a gallop. *Idiot. Ye've been bloody tricked.* The leather reins grew slick in his hands as he pushed Caraid faster. He'd left Alana alone and ignored his gut. Could there be any greater fool? He only prayed he reached her in time. He'd bet all his land Margot was with her. Hopefully Alana would put up a fight. Hopefully she wasn't dead already.

His heart felt like it had shrivelled at the thought. Instead of succumbing to despair, he allowed the boiling heat of anger to consume him. If she'd harmed her, by God...

Besides he was sure he'd know if Alana was dead. That strange connection they had would have told him, just like when the poison claimed her life.

The Old Castle came into view, the morning sun glinting over the top and forcing him to squint. Instead of seeming like a haven, the dark stone sent a dart of dread skittering through him. He studied the landscape but saw no sign of a horse. The muscles in his arms bunched. That didn't mean anything. Margot hadn't taken any mounts from Glencolum so she was likely on foot. He dismounted outside the crumbled walls and hooked Caraid's reins over a jutting piece of stone. He crouched low, easing his way around the walls until he came to the steps. Stealing another glance around, he crept up the steps and sucked in a breath as he drew his sword. A silent entry was impossible with the ancient oak door so he shoved it open quickly, blade out in front. His knees almost buckled as he spied Alana. Prone on the floor, hands and feet secured with rope, she released a muffled squeal through the material tied across her mouth as she spotted him. One cheek was red, her chemise filthy and tears filled her eyes.

Morgann barely noticed when Margot sprung from the shadows, a dagger held in one hand and a flaming torch in the other. He sniffed, the smell of oil strong in the air. A deep, agonising sickness pervaded through him as Margot grinned, torch held aloft.

"At last," she said. "We've been waiting quite some time, haven't we, Alana? I thought mayhap ye'd abandoned the woman ye love. A change of heart perhaps. But obviously not. Now if ye just lay down yer sword, we can get this over and done with."

He flexed his hand on the hilt. "Aye, ye come over here and I'll make it quick," he snarled.

"I wouldnae or she," she tilted her head toward Alana, "will go up in flames." She waved the torch around and Morgann's heart skipped as fire dripped and fizzled out on the wooden floor, too close to Alana's skirt for his liking.

"Nay!" He breathed deeply through his nostrils and eased the sword to the ground.

Alana released a muffled sound of protest but he ignored her, keeping his wary gaze on Margot.

"I thank ye, Morgann," she purred as she edged around him. "Now step over there." She motioned to the other side of the room with the dagger.

Morgann circled round, gaze darting between Alana and the flame. The heavy thump of his heart smacked against his ribs as the space between him and Alana increased. He longed to run to her, to drag her away from his vile stepmother but the fire dancing dangerously near to her thin shift prevented him. If he wasn't mistaken, oil stained the linen.

By God, Margot was out of her wits. Even though he'd known for a long time just how black her heart was, he could barely comprehend her wanting to burn Alana. The woman had always kept her distance from her misdeeds but it seemed she was ready to end it all by her own hand.

He swallowed heavily as his back bumped into the wall. This time she held the lass he loved hostage. A bitter tang filled his mouth. He couldn't lose her. Not like this. Alana was to die in his arms of old age, preferably together.

Margot pressed the dagger onto the table and reached for Alana, keeping a close eye on him and Morgann tensed his body, ready to snatch Alana from her at any moment.

"I thank ye, Morgann, for making this so easy on me. A few sweet words whispered in an ear and 'twas simple to find out where ye were. And then ye even abandoned poor Alana here to fend for herself."

Hauling Alana to her feet, Margot kept the torch dangerously close, the threat of the flame remaining as she crept toward the door. With her feet bound, Alana had to shuffle to stay upright while keeping herself from falling into the burning torch.

Alana's eyes were wide, fearful, and they clutched at his heart as he tried to communicate a secret promise to her. One that said he'd never let her come to harm, that he'd always protect her, that he'd die before letting her get hurt. He only hoped she understood how vital it was to him that she lived. For the first time in a long time, nothing else mattered. His lands, his family, his father... they were all inconsequential as long as Alana survived.

"Dinnae move," Margot warned as his feet twitched with the desire to lunge for his stepmother and wring her neck. "I'll put a torch to her, just ye see."

Margot inched open the door with her foot and pressed through the gap. Before her head disappeared behind the oak, she shoved Alana forward and flung the torch onto the rushes piled in front of the entrance. The door slammed shut as Alana sprawled to the floor and a blaze raced across the straw. Morgann jumped into action, snatching Alana away from the increasing flames and dragging her to her feet.

Assured she wouldn't fall over, he stomped on the growing blaze but they already consumed the oil soaked floorboards in a crackling, spitting mass of orange. He threw a desperate glance at Alana as the fire crawled up the door and blocked their exit.

The room filled with smoke. If the fire ate through the floor before they choked to death, they'd fall through to the basement and probably be buried alive. He snatched the abandoned knife and pushed Alana further back from the inferno. Her gaze remained on him, fearful, tear-laden as he sliced through her bonds, before kneeling and cutting through the ones around her legs. When he came to standing, he carefully untied the rag in her mouth. She remained quiet as the wooden floor popped and hissed. Each noise made her jump.

The agony tearing at his chest made his hands shake as he threw aside the gag and rubbed at the red marks it had left. Grease covered her shift and a bruise bloomed on one cheek. Her hair was mussed and dark circles rimmed her eyes. He swiped his thumb under her chin and gave her a half-smile. Morgann had never seen anything so beautiful.

"Ye shouldnae have come," she said as she wrapped her arms around him.

Closing his arms about her, he tucked Alana against him. He found himself surprisingly calm. He just needed to find a way for Alana to get out and all would be well. Everything moved slowly as the smoke swirled around them. The blaze completely covered the front door now and worked its way around the hall. The table would catch alight at any moment so he shifted Alana, arms still tightly around her, to the back chamber. There were no rear doors, no ramparts to escape to. This was a building intended as a home, not a fortress but the windows... He studied one. Aye, that could work.

"I wouldnae leave ye, *mo chridhe*, but ye have to leave me."

Her brow creased. "What is yer meaning?"

"The window." He nodded toward it. "'Tis wide enough for ye. I'll drop ye down and ye shouldnae hurt yerself. We're not that far up."

Alana blinked and stared at the window. "But... but ye'll no' fit through..." She shook her head furiously as she turned to him. "Nay. Nay, I'll not go."

"All will be well, I swear it. But ye must go, Alana. I'll find a way out myself."

A crack resounded through the hall, the sound of floorboards splitting and she flinched in his hold. Morgann urged her to the window as she clung to him and he carefully but firmly prized her arms away. "Go now, *m'eudail*, I willnae be long. I cannae find a way out if I'm worrying about ye now, can I?"

Alana released a tiny sob and swiped at her eyes. "Promise me ye'll no' leave me alone."

His throat felt tight and he didn't know if the moisture in his eyes was from the smoke or the thought of not holding her again. But he made the promise anyway. He would lie again and again if it meant she'd be safe. "I promise."

The prickling heat ate its way through the keep, the glow increasing as it consumed every fragment of wood in the building. By his reckoning, the floors would go first, then the wooden rafters holding up the roof. The castle didn't have long.

Cupping Alana's chin, he claimed a quick but powerful kiss from her. She trembled but Morgann knew she was holding back her fear, brave lass that she was. Ach, if he could only spend a little more time kissing her. But time he did not have.

He set her away decisively, deliberately schooling his expression. He refused to let her see how much the thought of leaving her was killing him. Each thud of his heart seemed to pound in protest. "Climb onto the windowsill and swing yer legs out. I'll lower ye down."

She didn't respond but did as he said, much to his relief. It was tight but she just managed to squeeze through at an angle and sit on the ledge. He grabbed her hands, pressed a kiss to each one. "I love ye," he murmured. "Now shuffle forward." Wriggling, she moved until perched right on the edge. He bunched his muscles. "Bend yer knees when ye land and ye'll be fine."

"I dinnae... Morgann, I—"

Before she could argue, he lowered her as far as possible. His shoulders wouldn't fit through the gap so he couldn't even see her as he did. She squealed and gripped him tight. With a sharp inhale, he released her. Her grip on him didn't last and he felt her go, listened for the thud as she landed but the sound of the raging fire meant he heard nothing. He only hoped she hadn't hurt herself.

Scrubbing a hand over his face, he turned from the window and stared at the door to the chambers. Flames licked at it. Aye, not much time at all. He studied the room, wracking his mind. He didn't want to leave her. He desperately wanted to keep his promise but it was hopeless.

He grinned as he slumped to the floor. At least Alana was safe.

***

Dirt bit into her hands as she landed and her feet stung with the impact but Alana was surprised she hadn't hurt anything else. She remained crumpled for a moment, her cheek pressed into the ground as the nausea in her stomach sapped her strength. She raised her gaze to the Old Castle. Smoke poured from the front windows and the main door had almost completely gone. Sitting, she took a steadying breath. Mayhap Morgann could get back through the hall and escape. A crash made her jump to her feet and she stumbled away to get a better view. A hand to her mouth, she gaped as fire danced out the top of the building.

The roof had fallen in.

Tears clouded her vision. Damn the man. He'd known he'd never get out alive. How could he leave her on her own? How could he promise her that all would be well?

A movement caught her eye and she turned toward the loch.

Margot.

Seething rage made her skin hot as she saw the woman, a wild smile on her face as she watched the keep crumble. The witch who had taken so much from her was now enjoying the sight of Morgann burning to death. Alana curled her hand into a fist until her nails bit into her palm and a wild cry tore from her as she raced toward her.

Margot only spotted her at the last moment as Alana

barrelled into her. The woman screamed and Alana knocked her down and snatched at her hair. She smacked a fist into her cheek as Margot tried to fend her off. She scratched at Alana's face, wriggling and clawing at her as they rolled to the water's edge.

Somehow Margot scrabbled to her feet and pushed Alana down into the water. She coughed as water seeped up her nose and into her mouth but she forced herself up and turned, kicking out at Margot. Alana gritted her teeth as the woman fell into the loch with a scream and she grabbed her skirts, hauling her close so she could bring a fist down on her again. Blood blossomed from Margot's nose and oozed down her face.

Dazed, Margot tried to crawl away but Alana kept a determined grip on her clothing, the fabric ripping as Morgann's stepmother tried to free herself.

"Ye willnae get away," Alana spat as Margot's thrashing drenched her in freezing water. "Ye've taken everything and I will make ye pay for what ye've done, I swear it."

Her fist throbbed, lungs ached but Morgann's face swam in front of her, images of their lovemaking plagued her, words of love lingered, and fired her anger as she pinned Margot beneath her, holding back her arms.

The dark-haired woman opened her palms. "Pray cease. Forgive me," she sobbed. "I'll no' fight anymore. Just dinnae hurt me."

Alana sucked in a long breath and studied the woman as the roar of the fire echoed in her ears. Loosening her hold on her wrists, she eased away. As much as she wanted to tear Margot apart, she couldn't bring herself to. Nay, the MacRaes could decide her fate.

But then she caught a glint of something in Margot's expression. A hint of a smile or a spark of triumph. Margot shoved suddenly at Alana but she reacted quickly, smacked her forehead into hers and knocked the woman out cold.

Sinking back into the water, Alana rubbed at her head and grimaced at the tender spot she felt. Margot floated at the water's edge and, with a sigh, Alana clambered out and dragged her onto the bank.

She lay across the pebbled shoal and finally released the sob that had been building inside her. Tears dripped down her face, mingling with the water from the loch. Behind her, the castle groaned as it surrendered to the flames.

She tried to control her ragged breathing but her chest ached too much. She may have lain there for only moments but time seemed to drift as her world fell from beneath her. She glanced over at the woman who had destroyed it. Somehow she needed to get her to Glencolum. Morgann's mount still waited for her master, tugging at her reins as if she knew what had happened to him. Alana swallowed the knot of grief trapped in her throat and came to her feet.

Her knees shook as she walked unsteadily to the horse's side and untethered her. She whinnied as Alana smoothed a palm over her muzzle and urged her over to the water's edge. Caraid obediently dropped to the ground while Alana dragged Margot over. The slender woman was not particularly heavy but her waterlogged clothes made it hard to lift her over the saddle. Alana took little care in hefting her over, taking bitter enjoyment in carting her around like a sack.

Palms pressed to her eyes, she blotted away fresh tears and inhaled deeply as she dug into Morgann's leather pouch and pulled some rope from it. She stroked the twine, remembering a time when it had been held in Morgann's hands, before tying it tightly around Margot's limp wrists. Hopefully that would hold her until Alana returned to Glencolum and Finn could ensure justice prevailed.

Even though it was painful to look at, she turned to eye the still burning remnants of the castle. Dust and smoke swirled about it, obscuring most of the ugly remains, the jagged beams and crumbling stone. How unfair it was that he'd been taken from her. Especially when she'd only just found him. A steady pain throbbed in her chest and exhaustion threatened to overcome her. Only the determination to see Margot held responsible for all she had done kept her standing.

She paused as she went to turn away and scowled as the smoke seemed to part. Her stomach flipped and she stumbled back a few paces, eyes wide. Nay, it couldn't be…

"Morgann!"

Alana sprinted toward him as he staggered from the ruins. His plaid was torn and smoke-stained, his face haggard, but he was definitely alive. She slammed into him and flung her arms around his torso as he reeled back under her weight.

"Yer alive!" she exclaimed as she buried her face into his chest. The stench of smoke filled her nostrils but she didn't care. Her tears seeped through the material as she burrowed her face closer, feeling the reassuring beat of his heart.

Strong arms came about her as he eased her away from the burning wreckage. He kissed the top of her head before pulling her back and resting his forehead against hers. Dirty thumbs rubbed away her tears as he drew in long breaths.

"Yer alive," she repeated quietly, unable to quite believe it. She clung tightly to him, fearful it was all some torturous dream.

"Aye."

"But how?"

Morgann kept hold of her face, his hands shaky as he recovered his breath. "I dinnae know." He shrugged and shook his head in disbelief. "I dinnae know."

They both glanced at the castle ruins. Most of the walls still stood but the insides had almost completely gone, smoke still pouring into the sky. Morgann turned to her and took her mouth in a desperate kiss. He tasted of charred wood and hope and love and she savoured it, knowing she would never let him go again.

A whinny from Caraid drew her attention and she let out a frustrated cry as she spied Margot righting herself in the saddle, hands still tied. She gave them a smug smile as she dug her heels into the horse's side.

"Margot," Morgann warned, his voice hoarse, "dinnae do it. Caraid willnae—" He cursed and released Alana as the mare bolted. He gave chase but it was too late. Margot spurred the horse on.

And then the mount veered toward the burning hulk of the castle as if led by an unknown guide. Margot fought to change course but Caraid was determined to take her into the inferno. Morgann stopped and gathered his breath as the mount and his struggling stepmother vanished into the smoke. Alana came up behind him and wrapped an arm around his waist as he chucked one over her shoulders and they waited.

Alana wasn't surprised when the horse trotted out of the mists riderless and unharmed but she still shook her head. "I dinnae know what we've done to deserve it, Morgann, but the spirits are with us."

Morgann twisted her into his hold as Caraid ambled over and began chewing on some grass as if nothing had happened. "Aye, it seems we do." He dipped his head and swept his lips over hers.

"I thought ye'd left me," she murmured against his lips as her heart swelled with relief and happiness. It was truly over and the gorgeous warrior was hers. She brushed her hands over his arms, tracing the indent of his muscles.

She felt him grin against her cheek as he squeezed her. "I told ye I'd not. Yer mine now, *mo ghràidh.*"

"Morgann MacRae," she raised her head and grinned back. "I've been yers since ye captured me."

***

Morgann pressed his sweaty palms against his plaid and glanced at Alana who gave him an encouraging smile as she stood next to her father. He noticed her squeeze a placating hand on his shoulder as Dougall flexed his fists.

He inhaled slowly as he moved past the other Campbells, who turned from their meals as he approached the main table. Shoulders straight, he kept his gaze fixed on Dougall even as he heard the faint scrape of knives as hands clenched around them. Ach, but he felt as though he were about to be thrown to the wolves. Still he was determined to do this properly.

Dougall remained sitting and Morgann stopped in front of the table and dipped his head. "My laird."

"MacRae," the older man greeted tersely.

"I have come to beg a truce on behalf of my clan." Morgann

found he had to force the words out and resist the urge to snarl. Only Alana's soothing presence kept him focused on why he was here. Today he would gain Alana's hand.

"Indeed."

He gritted his teeth. The old man wasn't going to make it easy on him. "Now that the woman who instigated the problems between the clans has been killed, there is no reason for us to continue hostilities. It would be beneficial for both sides if we joined forces." He flicked his gaze to Alana and had to stop himself from grinning. "And I'll like to join the clans permanently by taking yer daughter in marriage."

Dougall nodded slowly. "Alana tells me ye saved her from Margot. I'll always be grateful for that, but ye cannae expect me to give her to the man who kidnapped her surely?"

"I've made mistakes, just as ye have, Dougall."

The old man sighed. "Aye, mistakes were made. Alas, that woman's plotting got the better of all of us and I'll no' forgive myself for that. But my daughter is precious to me. I cannae hand her over to just anyone."

"Alana is precious to me too, Dougall. I'd die before I let anything happen to her. I swear it. And the MacRaes will forgive any wrongdoing on yer behalf, if ye let us be joined by marriage."

Dougall rubbed his chin as he studied him. Morgann resisted the desire to glance at Alana. He needed to stay focused on the task at hand. Lord knows the lass was a distraction.

"Da—" Alana prompted.

"Aye, aye," he said as he waved a hand at her. "I have need of a strong man to take care of Alana and I think it might be ye. I've got my reservations about this alliance but it seems... it seems I'm overruled."

Morgann would have laughed at the thought of such a man being overruled by a mere lass but knew well how persuasive Alana could be. And he didn't want to risk Dougall changing his mind.

"Then I have yer permission to marry her?"

"Aye, ye can marry my daughter and I'll negotiate a truce with yer clan. We are but old men and the fighting cannae continue. 'Tis time to forget the past, I think."

Grinning, Morgann nodded and allowed his gaze to drift to Alana. "I thank ye, laird. Ye'll no' regret it."

Alana beamed back at him, making his heart flip. "*I know,*" she mouthed at him.

Dougall held out a palm and Alana slid her hand into his. He passed her hand over to Morgann with a look that told him he'd better look after his daughter. Morgann grasped her fingers, the slim softness of her hand somehow sending a thrill through him.

"There ye go, MacRae, she's yours. Lord help ye..."

EPILOGUE

Tèile gripped the edge of the goblet and dunked her head into the wine, taking a long drink. Wiping her face with a hand, she grinned and eyed the couple at the main table as they whispered to one another. Oh aye, they'd been a pain but she couldn't help but feel a little fond of them.

Mayhap that was the wine talking...

But she was glad she'd aided them. And what a lot of help they'd needed. She was going to have to be very careful with her magic from now on. No doubt the *sidhe* council would ration it after she'd used some to help Morgann narrowly escape being crushed and to create a path through the fire. Though she'd not needed any magic to finish that vile Margot. Caraid had been more than happy to help rid the world of that woman.

She fluttered across the hall, enjoying the scent of roasted meats and the sound of drunken laughter. Both clans had gathered for the marriage of Alana and Morgann. Even Morgann's father had joined in with the festivities. Since the death of his wife, his health appeared much improved. Discovering the true nature of the manipulative woman seemed to have brought both lairds closer.

Tèile paused to scoop up a small handful of custard and licked it from her fingers as she tiptoed across the table in front of the couple. Aye, a job well done in her opinion. Now she could return to the land of the fae and celebrate properly.

The green faery jumped aside as Morgann slammed down his goblet and stood, drawing Alana into his hold. "If ye'll excuse me, I've a wife to see to."

Alana's cheeks turned crimson as she tucked her face into his neck and applause and shouts of approval rang out. Morgann swung her into his hold and men slapped him on the back as he carried her through the Great Hall and up the stairs.

Tèile couldn't resist following them and just having a little peek. In spite of herself, she was going to miss them. Before Morgann had a chance to slam the door shut with his foot, she flew in and settled herself on the windowsill with a sigh.

For all their problems, she thought, chin propped on a hand, *humans are very good at love.*

Morgann dropped Alana on the bed and she immediately wrapped herself around him, pulling him down for a demanding kiss. Tèile frowned when a tap at her shoulder meant she had to turn away.

"Tèile," said the faery, her purple gossamer wings sparkling in the sunset.

She brightened. It was time to go home!

"There is more work to be done here. Ye've used too much magic and now ye must put things right."

Tèile sagged against the stone, stealing one last glance at the couple as they stripped their clothes from one another and embraced.

"'Tis a love match again," the faery continued as she led her out of the window. "The man's name is Finn..."

The End

ABOUT THE AUTHOR

Samantha lives in a small village in Warwickshire with her husband, twin daughters and too many pets.. She writes full time, juggling motherly duties with Facebook. In her spare time, she likes to drag her tolerant family around castles.

www.samanthaholt.org.uk

56404028R00126

Made in the USA
Lexington, KY
21 October 2016